...d her ...

Alabama, with their one Amazing Child—who, fortunately, shows an aptitude for sports.

Visit Kimberly at **www.booksbykimberly.com** for the latest news—and don't forget to say hi while you're there!

THE POWER AND THE GLORY

BY
KIMBERLY LANG

All the characters in this book have no existence outside the imagination of the author, and have no relation whatsoever to anyone bearing the same name or names. They are not even distantly inspired by any individual known or unknown to the author, and all the incidents are pure invention.

First published in Great Britain 2011
by Mills & Boon, an imprint of Harlequin (UK) Limited,
Eton House, 18-24 Paradise Road, Richmond, Surrey TW9 1SR

© Kimberly Kerr 2011

ISBN: 978 0 263 88402 9

01-1111

Harlequin (UK) policy is to use papers that are natural, renewable and recyclable products and made from wood grown in sustainable forests. The logging and manufacturing processes conform to the legal environmental regulations of the country of origin.

Printed and bound in Spain
by Blackprint CPI, Barcelona

Also by Kimberly Lang:

THE PRIVILEGED AND THE DAMNED
GIRLS' GUIDE TO FLIRTING WITH DANGER
WHAT HAPPENS IN VEGAS…
BOARDROOM RIVALS, BEDROOM FIREWORKS!
MAGNATE'S MISTRESS…ACCIDENTALLY
  PREGNANT!
THE MILLIONAIRE'S MISBEHAVING MISTRESS
THE SECRET MISTRESS ARRANGEMENT

**Did you know these are also available as eBooks?
Visit www.millsandboon.co.uk**

To Marilyn Shoemaker, a true romance fan
and vocal advocate of the genre.
You are the kind of reader I always hoped to have.

And I must give special thanks
to my friend Frank Adams, who took time to answer
my questions about the workings of Congress while
en route to a meeting with the Speaker of the House.
For that display of awesomeness, I guess
I will now forgive him for not asking me to prom.

CHAPTER ONE

"*VIVE la Révolution.* Again."

Brady Marshall looked up from the text he was sending to see his father's chief of staff standing at the window overlooking Constitution Avenue. "What now?"

"A protest, but at least it's a small one. Maybe fifty people or so." Nathan shook his head. "Don't they have something better to do on a Friday morning?"

Nathan was a pessimist, a victim of too many years of D.C. politics. He was a good chief of staff in that Senator Marshall's office ran efficiently and smoothly, but he'd lost sight of the mission long ago. After this election, Brady would have to have a long talk with his father about the possibility of some fresh blood. "Maybe they paid attention to that 'engaged citizenry' part of their high school Civics class and decided to use this beautiful fall day to exercise their First Amendment rights to show their displeasure with…" *Any number of things.* "What's the protest about, anyway?"

"Does it matter?"

"Yes." Brady moved to the window, too. He couldn't hear the crowd, of course, but even from here he could see they were animated and engaged. "If I'm going to run that gauntlet, I'd like to know if they're upset over a recent policy vote or just my leather shoes."

"Why would you go out there?" Nathan went to his desk and opened a drawer.

"I'm meeting a friend on The Mall, and the shortest path is right through the middle of that group."

Returning to the window, Nathan lifted a small pair of binoculars to his eyes and focused on the crowd below. "I can't really tell for certain, but I'm betting tree huggers based on the signage."

"You keep binoculars in your desk?"

Nathan shrugged. "Came in handy today, didn't they?"

I really don't want to know. In this case, ignorance was most likely bliss. "Look." He stepped away from the window and started to gather his things. "The senator needs to look all of this over before we meet with the new consultant on Wednesday. If he wants to actively involve himself with strategy, that is. Otherwise, I'll take care of it."

Although this was his first time to officially spearhead a campaign, he'd been stumping for candidates his entire life, it seemed. He didn't particularly enjoy the daily grind of actual politics—and no matter what the speculations might be, he had no intention of ever running for the Senate seat his family had held for over forty years—but *campaigns*, on the other hand… Campaigns were a challenge.

Nathan nodded as Brady opened the door to the outer offices and waiting area. His father's staff and interns went about their business, greeting him as he made his way past. The waiting area was mostly empty, with only a few people waiting to see various members of the staff, and they were all actively staring at the young woman standing at the reception desk and speaking earnestly to the secretary. He stopped to see what was so engaging.

"Ma'am, you have to have an appointment." Louise's voice hit the perfect tone of patience and understanding while firmly standing her ground at the same time.

"I know, and that's why I'd very much like to *make* an appointment. I'm available at the senator's convenience." The woman had to be new at this. Not only did she not know there wasn't a snowball's chance in hell she'd get an appointment with his father, but it was also rather hard to take her seriously, dressed as she was. The form-fitting T-shirt belted over a long, free-flowing skirt, the tribal-looking jewelry and a riot of short brown curls held back from her face with a multicolored headband... Brady would lay money she was with the tree-huggers protesting outside. But if anyone seemed meant to carry off the cute-hippie look, this woman was it. She was slightly built, without looking fragile, with a profile that fell just short of elegant. She looked wholesome, fresh and perfectly suited to that particular fashion trend—all the way down to the Birkenstocks on her feet.

A collection of bracelets on her arm jangled as she punctuated her words with her hands. "As both a constituent and a spokesperson for the People's Planet Initiative, I'd like to offer the senator the opportunity to work with PPI and our members. Now is the perfect time for Senator Marshall to adopt a more aggressive stance toward environmental legislation and position himself as a leader in—"

Louise interrupted the torrent of words simply by holding up a hand. "Miss...?"

"Breedlove," the woman supplied. It was a rather traditional name for someone so nontraditional. He'd been expecting her to say something like "MoonChild."

"Miss Breedlove, this is a very busy week for the senator and his entire staff. There simply isn't time for anyone to meet with you—regardless of the merits of your organization's goals and mission," Louise qualified with a patient smile. "If you would like to contact us—say next week, through the proper channels?—we'll see about finding the appropriate member of the senator's staff to help you."

The woman's lips pulled into a tight frown. She'd finally realized she wasn't going to get much more than a polite brush-off. He felt a little bad for her. Having your passion slapped down by reality for the first time always hurt. "I see. May I leave some information for the senator to look over?"

Louise smiled now that she'd won. "Of course." As Miss Breedlove rummaged through a battered canvas bag, Louise directed her attention to him, and the smile turned apologetic. "Brady, I'm sorry, but I won't have my hands on the information you requested until tomorrow."

"No problem," he assured her. "We both know he's not going to look that over until ten minutes before the meeting anyway."

"Very true." Louise took the sheets of paper from Miss Breedlove as he left the office and the door swung closed behind him.

Louise was one of the loyal staff who'd worked with Granddad before he retired and stayed on when Dad won the seat. Brady had actually been surprised by her decision, since her years working alongside his family made her privy to much of their less-than-lily-white laundry. But, in the end, she'd put aside her personal dislike of Douglas Marshall the man for the sake of Douglas Marshall the senator and the greater good.

Just like he'd done.

"Mr. Marshall! Mr. Marshall, wait, please!"

He turned to see Miss Breedlove hurrying down the hallway at a near trot. *Uh-oh.* The elevator doors opened to an empty car, and the manners ingrained in him by Nana wouldn't allow him to step in and let the door close in her face.

"Thank you," she said as the doors closed and she tried to catch her breath. The quick run down the hall had added a touch of color to her cheeks and caused some of her hair to slip out of its containment to fall over her forehead. She was wearing little or no makeup, and her bright green eyes met his evenly. "Mr. Marshall," she began, "I'm with the People's Planet Initiative—"

"I'm sorry to interrupt, but I'm the wrong person for you to talk to."

"You're Brady Marshall, right? Senator Marshall's son."

"Yes, I am. But I'm not part of his office staff."

"I know. You're his campaign manager."

Miss Breedlove had done her homework. Brady wasn't sure if he should be impressed or slightly wary. "And as such, I have no control over his office calendar. I can't help you get an appointment with him."

"But *you* could listen to me, at least."

Since his good manners had him trapped in an elevator with the woman, Brady simply didn't know how to get around it. Not that Miss Breedlove was giving him a chance to.

"If Senator Marshall would embrace the mission of PPI, stand with us in *our* efforts, PPI's members could become valuable additions to *your* efforts to win his reelection. Our members are active and engaged in their communities—communities all over Virginia—and have a strong

Internet presence. You know how valuable grass-roots support is…"

Thankfully the doors opened on the first floor at that point, giving him the chance to dam the flood of words. "Louise has your information, and should your agenda prove—"

"We don't really have an agenda," she interrupted, and as he tried to move away, she trotted to keep up, talking the entire time. "We simply have a mission to make this planet a better place for all who inhabit it."

"That's admirable." *Be noncommittal.* He pushed open the doors to the outside and blinked at the sunlight.

Miss Breedlove was right behind him. *Still* talking. "With Senator Marshall's help—"

Ah, damn it. He'd walked right out in the direction of the protestors. With Miss Breedlove still talking a mile a minute in his ear about the "mission" of PPI, he watched as the protestors took note of her and then focused in on him. A second later, three broke away from the crowd and intercepted them on the steps.

Good Lord, he did *not* feel like dealing with this today.

"Mr. Marshall, if you'd just give me twenty minutes, I'm sure you'd agree that PPI's goals—" Miss Breedlove began, only to be interrupted by one of her people this time.

"The planet cannot continue to be exploited by this and every other government—" a man in a green T-shirt roared.

"We cannot stand idly by—" another woman added.

Brady tried to rein in his temper and exasperation as he cut them all off. "I appreciate your passion. And I'm sure you know that Senator Marshall has long enjoyed the endorsements of several prominent environmental groups for his strong support of conservation and other 'green' initiatives. But as I've told Miss Breedlove, I'm *not* the person you need to be talking to."

"I think you are," she said quietly as she placed her hand on his arm. Those big green eyes were earnest and engaging, and something about it nearly sucked him in. "Your family—as a whole—wields great influence and could really make a difference."

His family's influence. Yeah. That jerked him out of the depths of her eyes. "I'm very sorry, y'all, but I'm late."

The man in the green T-shirt stepped closer. "I'm sorry, too."

Before he could process Green Shirt's meaning, Brady felt something cold land on his wrist, followed immediately by the bite of metal into his skin. "What the—" He lifted his arm, only to lift Miss Breedlove's arm as well.

They'd been handcuffed together.

Green Shirt leaped down the remaining few stairs—shouting something about a talking tree?—and was swallowed by the crowd.

"Kirby! Come back!" she shouted, pulling at the metal on her wrist and jerking his wrist painfully in the process. "Unlock these things!"

The crowd went wild at that point, chanting and singing, somehow energized by the sight of their spokesperson shackled to another human being.

This is ridiculous.

Thankfully security arrived at the moment. In their excitement, the protesters had come too close to the building and needed to be pushed back to the proper distance. One of the officers, whom Brady had known for years, laughed as he walked over and saw his predicament.

"Did you want to be handcuffed to this lady? Should I be escorting you elsewhere?"

"Very funny, Robert. Just unlock the cuffs."

Robert leveled a stern look at Miss Breedlove. "You do understand that restraining someone against their will is a serious offence?"

Her eyes widened, and she tried again to slide her hand through the metal cuff. "I'm just as much the victim as he is. I didn't cuff us together."

"Can we sort out blame later?" Brady lifted their joined hands in Robert's direction, only to lower them quickly when he noticed the gathering crowd with cameras at the ready. "Maybe inside?"

Robert nodded, and pointed them back toward the doors.

The farcical nature of the situation was only exacerbated by the way Miss Breedlove tried to put as much distance between them as the handcuffs would allow, including contorting her hand into the most uncomfortable-looking position to avoid touching his. It didn't quite work.

Being handcuffed to this woman had at least accomplished one thing: she wasn't talking anymore.

Aspyn chewed on the inside of her lip as she followed Brady Marshall and the police officer back into the Russell Building. Not that she had a choice, thanks to Kirby's stupidity.

She might have to kill him for this.

Besides the obvious humiliation, Kirby's stunt was guaranteed to sour any goodwill she'd managed to garner from Brady Marshall and destroy her chances of ever getting an appointment with his father.

There was a time for showboating and a time for quiet

shows of strength—every activist who'd been around long enough knew that. Kirby was too new, too gung ho, to see that difference, and now she—and PPI—would be paying for it.

She kept her head high as the officer led them through the lobby and tried to keep as much distance as possible between herself and Mr. Marshall, who—thankfully—looked more exasperated than angry at the moment.

Chasing down Senator Marshall's son and campaign manager had been a whim; a whim, that, for a brief moment, she thought just might pan out. Now she needed to get out of these handcuffs and see if she could salvage anything at all from her efforts.

A door emblazoned with the Capitol Hill Police Force's emblem led to a small windowless room that looked suitable for interrogating suspects, and Aspyn wondered if she was about to get her first arrest on her record.

The officer—R. Richards from the name badge he wore—lifted their wrists and examined the cuffs. "Hmm. This is a problem."

"Why?" she and Mr. Marshall chorused.

He pointed to the locking mechanism. "These aren't standard handcuffs."

Mr. Marshall sighed, but Aspyn didn't understand the significance of the statement. "And?"

"*And* they don't take a standard key." Officer Richards gave her that stern look again, like this was all her fault or something. "Do *you* happen to have the key, miss?"

"No," she gritted out, "Because they're not my handcuffs. This was *not* my idea."

"Well, then we'll have to cut them off."

That brought another sigh from her cocaptive. The exasperation was starting to give way to something else. "And how long will that take?"

"Only a couple of minutes once I get the bolt cutters. *Finding* the bolt cutters will take a little longer, though."

Mr. Marshall finally looked at her fully—and the depths of his eyes caused flutters of something indescribable in her belly—and shook his head. He turned back to the officer and said, "I guess we don't have a choice. Go get the bolt cutters."

Officer Richards jerked his head in her direction. "Are you okay being left in here with her for a few minutes?"

Mr. Marshall looked her over and laughed, and she stiffened at the insult. "I think I'm safe enough."

They both kept talking like she wasn't even there, and Aspyn tried to keep her temper under control until the officer crossed to the door and made to leave. "Excuse me? Isn't anyone going to ask me if *I'm* okay being left in a windowless room, handcuffed to a complete stranger?"

"I can vouch for Brady. You'll be just fine."

And then they were alone. While she'd been half-kidding with her earlier statement, the reality of the situation hit hard. It was a small room, and Brady Marshall was quite a large man—almost a full foot taller than she was with really broad shoulders filling out a suit jacket that even she could tell was custom-made. And she'd felt the muscles in his arm when she'd touched him earlier. Since she couldn't get more than a literal arm's length away from him, she was now very familiar with the unique scent of his aftershave and the way his skin seemed to radiate warmth. Combined with a strong jaw, dark honey-colored blond hair that kept falling rakishly over his forehead and deep, leaf-green eyes... *Mercy.*

The worst part of this situation wasn't the public

humiliation or even the irritation she could tell Brady Marshall was keeping in check. No, the worst part was the fact that part of her didn't *mind* being handcuffed to him. He wasn't really her usual type… But on sheer looks alone, if she'd been asked to describe the kind of man she'd like to spend some quality time handcuffed to, Brady Marshall would do nicely. And now that they were alone… Granted, he kept looking at her like she belonged in a carnival side show, but her brain kept going to inappropriate places with those handcuffs. It was ridiculous, but that didn't stop the little tingly feeling low in her belly.

The silence was deafening. Aspyn sat on the table, letting her shoes fall off and her legs swing, and tried to relax the arm attached to his. To her surprise, Brady Marshall joined her on the table, allowing their hands to rest on the battered Formica top and releasing the strain caused by being cuffed to someone that much taller.

"How do you know it's safe to be left alone in here with me?" she asked. "For all you know, I could be a martial arts expert or something."

One dark blond brow went up as he took a long lazy look from the top of her head to the tips of her toes. It sent heat rushing to her skin. "Are you?" he asked.

"No," she admitted, "but you didn't know that."

The corner of his mouth quirked briefly. "Given the alternatives, it was a chance I was willing to take. And Robert has known me for years. He wouldn't have left you in here otherwise. I assure you you're in no danger from me at all."

Why did that feel a bit like an insult? "Good to know."

"Miss Breedlove—"

"Aspyn," she corrected.

That got her another of those side-show-oddity looks. "Excuse me?"

"I don't like to be called Miss Breedlove. My name is Aspyn."

His brow furrowed slightly. "Like the tree?"

She nodded. "Like the tree. Only it's spelled with a 'y' instead of an 'e.'" *He doesn't care about the spelling, you idiot.*

Understanding lit up his face, and he started to laugh. The laugh completely transformed his face, making him seem more real and less like a bureaucrat. The smile caused cute little crinkles to appear around the corners of his eyes. The complete change in demeanor was devastating to nerves already on high alert and helped blunt the force of having her name laughed at. "*Now* I understand why your friend was shouting something about talking to a tree as he ran off. I thought he was just crazy."

He wasn't laughing at me. That made her feel a little better. "He's not my friend. And I don't think Kirby's officially crazy, just a little overeager." She offered him a small smile. "I am really sorry about this, Mr. Marshall."

"All things considered, I think you should call me Brady." His mood seemed to be improving, and the nonfrustrated, nonexasperated Brady Marshall was a completely different person.

"Okay, Brady." She held out her hand to shake his, realizing a second too late *that* would be impossible for him. She let their hands rest on the table again and settled for, "Nice to meet you."

"You, too, although I wish the circumstances were bit different." A smile seemed to be tugging at the corners of his mouth. "I need to let my lunch date know I'm going to be late."

"Okay."

"I need my phone." There was definitely a laugh behind his voice, but she didn't get the joke.

"I'm right-handed." He indicated the cuffs that held them together.

She still didn't quite understand.

"So," he continued, "my phone is in my right pants pocket."

Understanding dawned. He couldn't reach it with his left hand, and if his right hand went into his pocket, her hand was going along for the ride.

"Oh." She felt her face heat. "Well, that's a little more personal than I thought we'd get today."

Amazingly enough, he winked at her. "Then I guess it's a good thing we're on a first name basis already."

She averted her eyes and tried to look unconcerned. Her arm brushed against his hip and her hand lightly touched his thigh as Brady slid his hand into his pocket—only to be stopped short wrist-deep by the cuffs. No amount of wiggling and maneuvering helped. The phone was deeper in his pocket than he could reach, but the pocket wasn't wide enough for both their hands and the cuffs to fit inside.

Brady cursed under his breath. "Do you mind just reaching in there and getting it?"

"Are you serious?" He wanted her to stick her hand down his pants? *No, just in his pocket,* she corrected.

As if in answer, his phone started to ring.

Her face felt like it was on fire and she cleared her throat. *No big deal. We're adults. It's a strange situation and we must work together. That's it.*

But sticking her hand in this man's pocket…?

Brady cleared his throat as a hint and angled his body toward hers as the phone continued to ring.

It was a bit of a contortionist's trick, causing her to twist her hand at an odd angle to slide it inside his warm pocket. She had to step close to him to accomplish the maneuver and being that close was quite overwhelming to her system.

She was careful to keep her hand as far to the outside as possible, but Aspyn couldn't help but notice the strong ridge of muscle that ran down his thigh. *What on earth did he do in his spare time to get thighs like that?*

Thankfully her fingers found the phone a second later, and she pulled it out quickly before her entire body combusted from embarrassment. Or other causes.

Brady's smile as she handed over the phone didn't help, and she turned away as he answered in a symbolic attempt to give him privacy. She was the one, though, that really needed that time to regain her composure. It was all she could do not to fan her face.

She overheard Brady laughingly tell someone he'd been unexpectedly detained and make a promise to explain and reschedule later.

"You okay, Aspyn?" he asked, putting his phone in his left pocket this time.

Pull it together. "I'm fine." *For someone who practically—if accidentally—just got to second base.* "I'm sorry to mess up your lunch plans."

"I believe you when you say this wasn't your idea. You might want to inform—Kirby, was it?—that the next person he handcuffs might not be as understanding."

"Does this mean you won't press charges?" Being arrested for trespassing or disturbing the peace—the normal charges protestors faced—was one thing. Unlawful restraint of a senator's son was a whole new level of trouble. And there was no way a judge would believe she was just an innocent bystander.

"Hadn't planned on it."

Relief washed over her. "Thank you. I promise I will personally wring Kirby's neck for this."

"I just don't know what he hoped to accomplish by it."

"It got your attention, didn't it?" Brady looked at her in surprise. "Do you know how hard it is to get someone's attention in this town? Especially when you're not already someone important?"

"I can imagine. But that justifies handcuffing people because…"

She didn't bother to try to hold back her frustration. "Our whole lives, we're told to get involved, only to find out that no one really *wants* us to. We're told to make our voices heard, but no one seems to be listening. And it's not just this protest or even just this organization. Most of us have been activists for years, and we found out pretty early on that no one really wants to hear what we have to say."

Brady nodded slowly. "I can imagine that's frustrating."

"Oh, it's more than frustrating," she snapped at his patronizing tone before she could stop herself.

"*But* a protest doesn't open lines of communication, either. It disintegrates into a matter of who can shout the loudest."

"*But,*" she countered, "we have to hope if we shout loud enough and long enough, someone might eventually hear us, because what we're saying *needs* to be heard. Have you seen what mountaintop mining does to Appalachia? What a rain forest looks like after it's been cleared? Have you ever cleaned oil off seabirds?" Brady shook his head.

"Well, I *have*. I know in your mind that might not justify this—" she shook their joined hands "—but I understand Kirby's intention. I don't approve, but I see his rationale and what motivated him."

He fell silent for a moment and Aspyn began to worry a little. Maybe she'd gone overboard. "I'll put in a good word for you with Louise. It won't get you a meeting with the senator, but it might—and I stress *might*—get you a meeting with someone on the staff."

"You'd do that?" Amazed didn't even begin to describe how she felt.

"Sure. But *not* because of this stunt," he clarified. "I don't want people thinking this is a good idea."

"Of course not. Thank you."

His face softened and those green eyes held dangerous warmth. "I can't guarantee anything, but someone with your passion and sincerity deserves a chance."

Wow. Aspyn didn't know which was more shocking— the idea she'd managed to at least get a foot in the door or the fact Brady Marshall thought she was passionate and sincere. The compliment tickled her down to her toes.

She'd seen Brady on TV campaigning with his father, and he always seemed rather aloof and unapproachable. *This* man, though, was so *not* what she expected. When he smiled at her again, the tickle became a tingle, and the reminder she was handcuffed to him and alone in a windowless room came rushing back.

Complete with full-color visuals.

She cleared her throat. "I, um—"

Officer Richards returned then, sparing her from saying something stupid. "We get more sit-ins than handcuffing, so I don't get to use these much." He worked the giant handles experimentally.

Brady stood and pulled up the sleeve of his coat and unbuttoned his cuff to roll it back out of the way. "Not exactly the confidence I was hoping for. I'd like to keep my wrist attached."

The officer just grinned. "Who's first?"

"Ladies first." Brady moved their arms to the center of the table. "Aspyn?"

She pushed up her sleeve and slid her bracelets up, away from the metal cuff. "I'm not sure I want to be first. I like my wrist, too."

Despite the banter between the men, Officer Richards handled the bolt cutters with ease and soon her wrist was free. She rubbed the red mark circling her skin as another squeeze of the enormous handles let Brady pull his wrist free as well.

Brady moved on immediately, rebuttoning his cuff and shaking the officer's hand. Whatever "moment" they'd shared, it was over now, and Brady was back to the rather stiff and aloof man she'd jumped in an elevator with. It seemed a shame, like a loss. "Thanks. Unless you need something from me…" Officer Richards shook his head. "Good. Bye, Robert. Aspyn, it's been…interesting meeting you."

"And you. I hope the rest of your day is uneventful."

"That would be nice." Then Brady was gone, and the room felt big and empty.

Aspyn grabbed her bag and inched toward the door. "Have a nice day, Officer—"

"Not so fast."

Thirty uncomfortable minutes later, Aspyn was able to leave with Officer Richards's warnings still ringing in her ears. The man certainly didn't like scenes in his building or on the steps.

Most of the protestors had dispersed and only a few hard-core activists remained with Jackie, the head of the People's Planet Initiative and the protest organizer. Even they seemed to have lost much of their energy, though. She waved as she came down the steps, and Jackie crossed the street to meet her. "I videoed the whole thing. It was brilliant. Your parents are going to be so proud."

"You think?" That brought a smile to her face. Living up to her legacy didn't seem quite so daunting at the moment.

"I *know*. I'll upload it and you can send them the link."

"They're still doing recovery in Haiti. They're not exactly in a WiFi hotspot most of the time."

"Well, you'll be able to show it to them eventually. Their little girl's first time." She held up the small video camera. "So, Aspyn Breedlove, how did it feel to leave a protest in handcuffs?"

She frowned into the camera. "It wasn't like that, Jackie. It was a stupid stunt, and Kirby was way out of line."

"But you got someone's attention. That's a great first step."

"Maybe. Maybe not. But it's made me hopeful. Eventually, maybe someone will start listening to us. That's all I really want." Jackie raised an eyebrow at her. "Okay," Aspen corrected, "so it's the start of what I want—what we all want. Someone to actually listen to us."

Jackie turned off the camera. "Go on home. You've done enough here today."

Aspyn thought about Brady's offer to help. "We'll see, I guess." At Jackie's confused look, she added, "I'll explain later." No sense getting into any of that and getting anyone's hopes up until it came to pass.

As she headed to the Metro station, the absurdity of

the day finally hit her. In all honesty, there wasn't that much to explain—beyond the fact she'd found out that Brady Marshall was devastating up close, and she certainly wasn't sharing *that* information with the public. Even if she happened to get a meeting with someone in his dad's office, she still couldn't share the how. Not that anyone would believe her anyway...

She settled into the seat for the trip out of the city, proud of herself for what little she might have managed to accomplish today. It wasn't much, but it was a start. *One step at a time.*

The familiar sway and rattle of the train lulled her and she closed her eyes. Brady Marshall's face was waiting for her. A little sigh escaped before she could help it. But then that warm feeling returned to her chest.

She was passionate. She was sincere.

And forty-eight hours later, she was an Internet phenomenon.

CHAPTER TWO

"You getting handcuffed to a hippie is just priceless. I took a screen shot and made it the wallpaper on my desktop. And Finn had one of his editing guys recut and redub it and it's hysterical. I'll send you the video."

Brady could barely understand Ethan through the laughter. He leaned his head against the seat back as the limo inched its way through traffic and pinched the bridge of his nose to fight back the rapidly growing headache.

This was the final straw. He wasn't answering his phone again today. Brady had already dealt with the press, his grandparents and the chair of the party's Senatorial Reelection Committee because some half-cracked tree-hugger decided to pull a stupid stunt. A video of the event had gone viral overnight, and the voice-over of Aspyn saying, "It's all I want… Someone to actually listen to us," had become a rallying cry for every frustrated activist in the country. By Monday, she was everywhere on the Internet; by Tuesday, the press had really caught on and doubled-down on their coverage. The bloggers and pundits were eating it up, and Aspyn was now the figurehead of a movement that hadn't existed three days ago.

And he'd been dragged into it as the symbol of old-school, establishment politics. It didn't seem to matter *he* wasn't a politician; he could listen all day long and it wouldn't make a bit of difference. As a Marshall, his name alone was all they needed to make their point.

He'd be drawing on what little patience he had left just to get through the meeting with his father and the new campaign consultants. He had none to spare for his brothers—either of them. "It's not half as interesting as the talking heads make it out to be."

"But it's still funny. Oh, and Lily wants me to remind you that at least *she* never made the handcuffed 'walk of shame' on the national news."

Ethan's fiancée had an extensive juvenile record that, for the most part, they'd managed to keep from becoming blog fodder. Not that Ethan cared one way or the other— not who knew about Lily's past nor what trouble it might cause politically to have a former delinquent in the family. Lily was nice enough, and he was glad his brother was happy, but she'd caused more than one headache for him already. "Is there an actual purpose for your call, Ethan?"

"Not really." Brady could almost hear Ethan's shrug. "Just wanted to annoy you."

"You succeeded."

"So, out of curiosity, *did* you listen to her?"

"Sort of. I told her I'd try to get her a meeting with one of the staffers. She seemed happy enough with that until all this broke loose."

"She's tapped into something in the people's psyche. You're practically getting wall-to-wall coverage."

Like he didn't know *that* already. "People are frustrated with the system. What's new about that? On an otherwise slow news day, a pretty girl riding Internet-fueled fame makes the headlines. This will pass." *Hopefully very soon.*

"So you think she's pretty?"

Sometimes Ethan could display stunning acts of immaturity strictly to try to get a rise out of him. Today was not a good day to take the bait. "Does it matter?"

"I wouldn't have thought you'd go for the whole anti-establishment, counterculture type. She falls outside your norm—and you *never* fall outside your norm."

The headache behind his eyes throbbed. "Must you be a complete idiot all the time?"

"You didn't answer my question."

"Because you're being an idiot." The limo pulled to a stop at his father's town house. "And I now have to go do damage control on this. Campaign staff should not be getting more air time than the candidate."

"Uh-oh, sounds like the senator's a little upset about this." Ethan didn't bother to cloak his bitterness. "Good."

"Maybe for you, but not for me. I'd rather not be wasting time spinning ridiculous press. *I'm* the one who has to get him reelected."

"It was your choice to work for him."

"Yes. Because I can see beyond my own petty interests and childhood issues best worked out with a therapist."

Ethan muttered something under his breath, but Brady wasn't interested and hung up after a terse "goodbye." Ethan couldn't get past his own problems with their father to see the bigger picture. Douglas Marshall might be a lousy excuse for a father, but he was a damn good senator. Granddad's legacy, oddly enough, was in good hands.

And that's what was important, even though Ethan couldn't see it. The mission that drove his family was coded into his DNA. Granddad had been a lion in the Senate, a forceful voice and advocate. Their father was carrying on that tradition, and as long as that was the case, Brady would fight to keep him in that seat.

Which meant he needed to turn the attention away from Aspyn Breedlove and back to the issues that really meant something.

He climbed the steps two at a time and let himself in. To his right, the door to his father's study stood open, and he could hear voices inside. As he entered, he was surprised to see his father, Nathan and the new consultants already seated around the shiny conference table. And from the used coffee cups, open laptops and untidy stacks of paper, they'd been there for a while.

"Am I late?"

Jane, one of the consultants he'd brought on board only last week, had the good grace to look slightly abashed. Nathan just shrugged. His father, though, looked irritated, as always.

"Your little hippie friend has created quite the stir—"

"It will pass."

"Possibly, but I'm sick of seeing her face—and yours—every time I turn on the news." As if to prove his point, his father grabbed the remote and turned the sound up on the television. There, on one side of a split screen, was the video of Aspyn trotting beside him as they left the building and then being handcuffed to him. On the other side was a shot of an online bulletin board railing against the deafness of Congress and organizing itself into a full-fledged protest. The perky anchorwoman delivering the commentary called it a "grassroots uprising" and mentioned the Marshalls at least five times like it was somehow *their* fault.

The image then switched to Aspyn giving a make-shift press conference inside of what looked like a small bookstore. "I think the reaction we're seeing just proves I'm not the only one frustrated with the disconnect our

lawmakers have from the people they're supposed to represent. Everyone deserves to be heard." It wasn't the first
time he'd seen the clip, and, once again, he was impressed
with how natural and articulate Aspyn was on camera. She
might be a little out there, but she was smart and well-spo-
ken and could hold her own with the press.

His father muted the sound again. "Because Miss
Breedlove decided to handcuff herself to you, *my* office
is now the center of this storm. Suddenly I'm the poster
child for all that is wrong in Washington."

Jane looked up from her computer as Brady joined them
at the table. "And Mack Taylor is already keying in on it,"
she added. "It's about to become a campaign issue, and
with the Marshall name prominently connected to the uprising, it doesn't reflect very well on the senator."

If I'd just let the elevator doors close in her face... Good
manners didn't always pay off, it seemed. But, then this
was also what made campaigns exciting and challenging.
This, too, just needed the right spin, and his brain was
churning with the challenge already.

"Don't get comfortable, Brady." His father interrupted
the thought. "You're going on a little field trip."

His brain screeched to a stop. That didn't bode well.
"Where and why?"

"I need to make Miss Breedlove my friend before Mack
Taylor can make her my enemy and use her against me."

"That's always a good plan. In fact—"

"I'm glad you agree. You're going to hire her."

He couldn't have heard that correctly. "Excuse me?"

"You are going to hire Miss Breedlove and make her a
part of our campaign staff."

That was the most ridiculous thing he'd ever heard.
"Doing what, exactly? Protesting?"

"Listening." His father smiled smugly. "Miss Breedlove is going to be my official Campaign Listener."

No, *that* was the most ridiculous thing he'd ever heard. "That's not a real job."

"It is now. Instead of calling my office, concerned and engaged citizens may contact Miss Breedlove, who will listen to their concerns and organize them so they can be presented to me."

That headache started to throb again. "You're not serious."

"Oh, yes, I am. That should keep Miss Breedlove busy and off the cable news networks, and it will show that I am attentive to the concerns of the people and want to give them a point person to contact."

"And anyone with an ounce of sense will see it for the ploy it is. This isn't a campaign issue. Listening and replying to constituents is a job for one of your staffers."

Jane shook her head. "It's a ploy, but it's a ploy that will work."

"This was your idea, wasn't it?" He pinned her with a stare that had her squirming slightly before she nodded.

"Since you're the one she handcuffed herself to, you're the one who needs to be seen listening to her first."

"And when the campaign is over?" he asked his father.

"Miss Breedlove can go back to whatever cause brought her to my office in the first place."

Meaning he's not going to listen to a single thing she has to say. This was more than just a ploy. It was a step above an empty publicity stunt. It was inherently dishonest and that bothered him. They were above this kind of trick. "I get the impression Aspyn is a true believer. She's going to expect this to be an honest offer. When she finds out it's not, the backlash could be staggering."

"It is an honest offer," his father supplied. "Of a job. Beyond that, we make no guarantees, so we're not being dishonest in any way."

Political splitting of hairs. "Only in spirit."

His father sighed. "Good Lord, Brady, you sound like Ethan and his quest for truth and justice. You understand the bigger picture. Just find the girl a desk and let her channel her energies in a different direction."

Brady tried one last attempt at reason. "If we do this, it sets a dangerous precedent and every activist in the country will find a politician to handcuff themselves to."

"It's a risk I'm willing to take." He nodded at Nathan, who shoved papers across the table at Brady. "Mary Aspyn Breedlove, age twenty-seven, foreign-born to American parents but raised in the U.S. in a variety of hippie-type communes. Some college work—mainly in Sociology before she dropped out to annoy people full-time—and a long history of do-gooding and activism. Miss Breedlove has no criminal record and a current address in Arlington. I'm sure you'll enjoy working with her."

In other words, Aspyn was officially his problem now.

Aspyn peeked out of the blinds and groaned. Still there.

She flopped back onto the futon and heard it creak ominously in protest. *Ugh.* She felt like a prisoner. The video had gone viral with a speed she couldn't wrap her head around, and the nation had arrived on her doorstep shortly thereafter. Technically it was Margo's doorstep, since she lived above Margo's bookstore. The bookstore was hopping now, and Margo was thrilled with the free publicity and additional business Aspyn's new notoriety brought— even if Aspyn herself had to take time off and Margo's niece brought in to help instead. From her tiny apartment on the second floor, Aspyn could watch the crowds and the press mill around out front. A small demonstration was organizing across the street, showing support for this new "movement" she supposedly—if completely accidentally—started.

She should be proud of what she'd accomplished— especially since it had required so little effort on her part. This kind of attention was every activist's dream, but sadly, it wasn't quite for the reasons she'd hoped for when she chased down Brady Marshall.

She'd turned her phone off last night, put an autoreply on her email account and settled in to wait it out. Thankfully the stairs up to her apartment were in the back room of the bookstore, so at least no one was knocking on her door.

Except that someone was...

She rolled off the futon ungracefully and crossed to the door, wondering who Margo had let up. Whoever it was, she hoped they brought food with them. And, to be honest, she was a little bored and could use some company.

Confusion reigned when she opened the door to find Brady. Here. At her door. *Why?*

"Mr. Marsh—I mean, Brady. Hi." She ran her hands over her hair and tried to smooth down the curls. *Be casual.* "What brings you here?"

"I came to talk to you."

Was that a good thing or a bad thing? "Okay."

Brady smiled, adding a heart stutter to her body's strange reactions to his presence. "Could I come in?"

I'm such an idiot. "Of course. Please." She stepped back and held the door open. As Brady moved past her, that scent that she remembered so well tickled her nose and she inhaled deeply.

He seemed relaxed and unconcerned, unlike the man

she'd seen on TV the last couple of days. At the moment, he didn't seem angry about the media firestorm raging around him, but why else would he be here? "I was a little confused to find a business at your address. I guess it's convenient to live above where you work."

"It is. And it's cheap," she added with a small laugh. "I'm sorry about the mess." She skirted around him to grab an armful of clothes and books off the futon and tossed them into the closet. "I've been rather homebound."

"Since I just fought my way through that crowd, I fully understand why you're hiding up here."

"I would think your arrival here would only stir them up more."

"Oh, it did." He didn't elaborate, but his face showed his exasperation with the situation.

Yeesh. Did that mean she was about to get an earful?

"Please, sit. Can I get you something to drink? Juice? Water? Herbal tea?" *Stop babbling*. She just couldn't get her head around the fact Brady was *here*. The only people more confused about his presence would be the reporters outside.

He looked completely out of place, sitting on her rickety futon in his impeccably tailored suit and conservative red power tie surrounded by colorful batik cushions. Slivers of sunshine peeking through the slats of the blinds refracted through the glass beads of her curtain and sent tiny rainbows dancing over his skin.

Brady declined her offers with a small shake of his head. He seemed completely relaxed, leaning back and balancing one ankle on his knee. "It's a bit of a circus out there."

His mild, conversational tone didn't help her relax any as she perched on the opposite arm of the futon, as far away physically as she could be without sitting on the counter of her kitchenette. "Definitely. I mean, I'm glad people are trying to find their voices, and that the media is showing that search and desire, but I wish…"

The corner of his mouth turned up. "They'd do it somewhere else?"

"Exactly." She sighed. "Is that terrible of me?"

"Not at all. You didn't ask for the spotlight."

"And I don't want to be there. There are so many issues that deserve at least half the media attention *I'm* getting just because Kirby was an idiot. It's amazing what passes for news."

He chuckled, and the sound caught her off guard. "I told the senator you were a true believer."

He had spoken to his father about her? Not just some random staffer, but the senator himself? Wow. But the humor in his voice put her on guard a little. "You make that sound like a bad thing."

"No, not at all…" Brady trailed off, and she realized his attention had been caught by the photo on the side table.

"Those are my parents," she supplied when he picked up the frame and stared at it, surprise on his face.

"Are they actually handcuffed to the White House fence?"

"Yes, they are. If you look over my dad's shoulder, you can see the top of my head. He had me in a backpack."

An eyebrow went up. "Baby's First Protest?"

"My third, actually."

Brady replaced the photo, shaking his head at it as he did. "So it runs in the family."

"Oh, no. They handcuffed themselves to the fence intentionally."

He shook his head. "I meant the activism."

"That? Oh, yes. My parents have always been

activists—antiwar, environmental issues, Civil Rights—all kinds of good causes. I don't remember which protest that particular one was, but that time they made the papers with that photo."

"You're telling me they handcuffed themselves to the White House fence more than once?"

Brady's shock was amusing, but she stifled the laugh. "Yeah. They really are what you'd call 'true believers.' They've made a difference."

"What do they have to say about all of this?" He jerked his head toward the crowd outside.

"They were pleased to hear about it, but they don't know how big and out of hand it's gotten now." At his look, she added, "Communication is sporadic at the moment. They're in Haiti doing relief work."

"They sound like good people."

Pride filled her. "They are. The best, actually. I wish I had their dedication."

"You don't?"

No, to their everlasting shame. "My parents have devoted their lives to something much bigger than themselves. They want to make a difference, and that involves sacrifices. Surely you understand that better than most."

A crease formed across Brady's forehead. "What do you mean?"

"Your family is in politics. They've dedicated themselves to public service, to the greater good." Brady seemed to find that amusing. "Even with all I know, I'm still an optimist at heart. That's why I do what I do. I *hope* that's also what draws people to politics—that need to try to make a difference."

Brady paused at her words. "In theory, yes. In practice… Well, it varies."

"Then that's all the more reason for the people to find their voices and make themselves heard. I hope that's what all this—" she waved her hands toward the window "—leads to. More communication—open dialogue and real listening—between the people and their elected officials."

"And that segues nicely into why I'm here."

Oh, yeah. She'd forgotten there had to be a purpose for his visit—a purpose she probably wasn't going to like. Once again, she'd been sucked into conversation with Brady and forgotten to focus. That was a shame really—having to focus on a topic—because she found she really liked talking to him. She knew he found her to be odd and slightly amusing, but Brady was easy to talk to. *Looking at him wasn't bad, either,* a little voice inside her piped up, but she quickly shushed it and braced herself. "Okay, I'm listening."

The corner of Brady's mouth quirked up. "Good. Because that's exactly what I want you to do."

"Listen to you?"

"No. The public at large."

She must have missed an important point somewhere. "I'm sorry, I'm not following you."

"I'm here to offer you a job."

Aspyn nearly fell off her perch in shock. Surely Brady was kidding. She studied his face and realized he was serious. *Wow.* "But I already have a job. More than one, in fact."

"I hope you'll consider taking a leave of absence from all of them and come to work for me." He cleared his throat. "For the campaign, that is."

Had Margo slipped some salvia into her coffee this morning? If this wasn't a hallucination, then… *Whoa.* "I…

um…I mean." She stopped and cleared her throat. She still had a chance to salvage this situation—if she could manage to keep her wits and professionalism around her. "That's very kind—and intriguing—but I don't know anything about campaigns."

"You don't need to. That's my job." She started to interrupt, but he held up a hand. "And you seem very bright. I have no doubt you'll catch on quickly."

Why did compliments from Brady make her feel all warm and sparkly inside? "I really don't want to work for a political campaign. That's not the kind of activism I'm interested in."

"I would argue that it is, in a way." He leaned forward and braced his elbows on his knees. "Senator Marshall would like you to listen to the people. Those that want to make their voices heard would contact you through the campaign. You'd keep track of what issues matter most to people and prepare recommendations for us on the issues you feel we should be embracing."

"Are you serious?"

"Very much so. If nothing else, this has proven to the senator and his staff that people are very frustrated and feel silenced. He wants to be the senator known for really listening to his constituents."

That sounded good in theory, but she probably wasn't the right person for the job. "I don't have any experience…"

"I beg to differ. Your work in the Peace Corps, community organizing, the activism… You've proven you really care, and that's what really matters. I'd say you were ideally suited for this kind of job."

How'd he know so much about her? "Did you run a background check on me or something?" Every warning her parents had ever given about government invasion of the privacy of the citizenry echoed in her ears. Maybe they weren't just being paranoid after all.

"Yes."

And obviously he didn't see that as a problem. "I don't know—"

"It will also shut down that circus outside and refocus their attention."

That would be nice. "How?"

"You are their cause célèbre. Once you have the ear of Senator Marshall, they can't use you as a martyr or poster child anymore. Therefore, much of this will lose its steam. One press conference—"

"Whoa, a press conference?"

He nodded. "First thing in the morning to announce your new position."

Aspyn couldn't find words. Her mouth was moving, but nothing was coming out. She gave herself a hard shake. "You're not giving me much time to think about it."

"It's the first rule of campaigns, Aspyn. Move quickly."

She stood and walked over to the sink for a drink of water. "I don't know, Brady. I'm not really comfortable with the idea." *For many reasons.*

The futon creaked, meaning Brady was on his feet now, too, but she didn't expect to feel his hand on her arm. It sizzled like a brand against her skin, and the sizzle spread outward over her body like a ripple across a pond.

And that gave her another reason—a very good one—to be uncomfortable with the possibility of working for him. She could very easily develop inappropriate ideas about Brady Marshall. She already *had*, she reminded herself; she just hadn't had much time to ruminate on those ideas due to the current melee of her life. But they were there, poking at the edges of her mind, springing out in full color at inopportune moments and being explored in-depth in some pretty explicit dreams involving those handcuffs.

"Why not do it?"

For a split second, she thought Brady had read her mind and meant do *it*. Then sanity returned. When she turned, Brady was way too close for comfort, and she found herself staring directly at that broad chest. With the counter at her back, there was no room for retreat, and she sidestepped around him for much-needed distance.

Why did this apartment have to be so small?

"Well…" She searched for a good reason, one Brady might buy. The sight of him in his suit standing beside her salt lamps and crystals gave her one. "I'm rather *anti*establishment, if you can't tell. Working *for* the establishment just might cause a cognitive dissonance that would make my head explode." *And give my parents a heart attack.*

This time, Brady's amusement irritated her. "Ah, well, think of it as an infiltration, then. Think about all the inside information you'll learn that can be used *against* the establishment sometime in the future."

Now she was getting suspicious as well. "You seem rather keen on me taking this job. Why?"

"I wouldn't have offered it to you if I wasn't."

She crossed her arms over her chest. "What's in it for you?"

"Me, personally?" He shrugged. "As the manager of this campaign, I want to win this election. This will help. *You* can help. Everyone wins, in fact—me, you, Senator Marshall and the good people of Virginia."

Guilt about her suspicions nibbled at her. Other than the fact politics was full of professional liars, she had no real reason to distrust Brady personally. He could have made a big deal of Friday's escapade, let her be arrested, but he didn't. Instead he'd offered—and it seemed delivered—the chance to make her case to the senator's office. Now he was giving her the chance to make a small difference *and* get this mess cleared up.

But to work for the brick wall she'd been slamming against her entire life…?

It was only a temporary position. The election was just a little over five weeks away. It wasn't like she was selling her soul to the devil. If it didn't work out, she hadn't really lost anything. It wasn't like the political establishment could ignore her *more* than they already were. And if it did work out like Brady said… Well, something good might be gained.

And her parents? *That* was going to be an awkward conversation. But they were in Haiti for the foreseeable future. All of this could be over with long before they got back and ever had to know about it. Why couldn't she work for change from the inside for a while? If she was successful, she'd tell them all about it. If not…

"Well?" Brady prompted.

Which brought her right back to the very personal problem she had with this opportunity. Could she work with Brady and not drool over him every day? Could she avoid a silly office crush egged on by her overactive imagination? Of course, there was the distinct possibility that as low man on the campaign totem pole, she'd have little interaction with Brady at all. And while the thought made her want to stamp her foot in frustration, realistically, that might be for the best.

Seems like I've talked myself into it. "All right. I'll take the job."

* * *

Aspyn still looked at him with equal parts suspicion and amusement, which didn't fully surprise him. What *did* surprise him was the brief moment when she'd let that mask slip and sized him up like a yummy treat she'd like to devour but knew she'd regret the calories later. It was the echo of that same sentiment in *him*, though, that had him wanting to retract the offer and look for a plan B approach out of this PR mess.

"Okay, then. Press conference tomorrow morning at ten." He eyeballed the battered and body-hugging jeans and nubby cardigan she wore and considered discussing a dress code. Then he looked around her apartment and decided it wasn't worth his breath. The campaign had their official granola earth-mother on staff and she would probably look the part. "I'll send a car for you at nine."

One eyebrow went up. "You'll send a car? Where is this press conference going to be?"

"Campaign HQ, of course."

The other eyebrow joined the first. "That's less than a mile from here."

"And?"

"*And* I can walk or ride my bike." Aspyn crossed her arms over her chest. "The first issue I'd like to bring to your attention is the waste of resources that things like 'sending a car' are—both to the planet and the campaign."

He bit back the sigh as Aspyn started in on an obviously often-delivered speech.

He really was going to regret this.

CHAPTER THREE

MARGO was in the process of opening the store when Aspyn came down Thursday morning, ready to tackle her first day of work—even if she still wasn't one hundred percent clear on what she'd actually be doing.

"Good morning!" Margo sang out. "Don't you look adorable?"

Aspyn tugged at the borrowed black skirt. "You think?"

"Definitely. And not just adorable, either. Competent. Capable. Professional. You're going to knock 'em dead." Margo was a proponent of dressing for the part. As the owner of a New Age bookstore, she leaned toward caftans and head scarves, even when the result was more "carnival fortune-teller," because that's what people expected. She'd been the driving force behind Aspyn's wardrobe today, practically manning a phone tree to find all the appropriate pieces. "Here." Margo passed her a travel mug with the bookstore's logo on it. "A ginseng and kava tisane to get you going today."

Margo mothered her unreservedly, and Aspyn was thankful for it today. She needed the cheerleading. The events of the last few days had her head spinning as it was, but yesterday… She couldn't quite decide what had her more off balance: Brady's offer, the fact she'd accepted it, or her disturbing reaction to Brady himself. About midnight last night, she'd finally convinced herself she'd be able to handle this job and keep her hormones under control.

The bags under her eyes rather belied that already shaky resolve.

"Now go. You don't want to be late for your press conference."

"I feel terrible leaving you short-handed, with no notice—"

Margo waved a hand. "Annabelle will do fine, and my sister is glad to have her doing something other than lazing around the house. This is an amazing opportunity for you, honey. Take it." Then she leaned in with a coy smile. "And the scenery there is much better than anything you'll get around here."

"The scenery?"

"If you must take a job in the political machine, eye candy like Brady Marshall makes it go down much easier." Margo fanned herself, causing an armful of bangles to jangle. "I'm considering volunteering for the campaign myself."

"Don't be silly." Margo wasn't really helping in the it's-not-about-Brady-Marshall department. "Anyway, he's the campaign manager, and very, very busy, I'm sure. I doubt I'll have much interaction with him at all. Other than the press conference today, I bet I'll rarely see him." *Bummer*.

"Pity." Margo patted her arm, adjusted her necklace and unlocked the front door. "Go. Have a great day."

The neighborhood was awake, bustling but not too busy. After the media circus of the last few days, it was nice to see things getting back to normal. Brady had made an announcement to the media on his way out yesterday—she hadn't heard it, but it had worked wonders. Only a few cameras were still hanging around, but she had no doubt they'd be out in full-throng at HQ.

Once she was safely around the corner and out of sight from the bookstore, Aspyn sipped carefully from her mug. Her eyes watered and she ducked into the coffee shop. Joe, the owner, held out his hand, and she handed over the mug without comment.

Joe dumped the tisane into the sink, refilled the mug with the French Roast she preferred and gave it back with a smile.

"Thanks, Joe. You're awesome."

"Margo means well."

"I know. And I love her for it. Nothing beats caffeine, though." She inhaled the steam gratefully before putting the lid back on. "And I'm going to need it today."

Joe waved away her money. "It's on me. Good luck."

He turned to another customer, and she waved goodbye. She'd built in plenty of time to make the walk, but the shot of caffeine mixing with nerves already on edge had her covering the distance in half the expected time. Sure enough, there were press vans outside HQ. Not as many, she noted, as yesterday. Had the press already lost interest?

Aspyn took a deep breath to steady herself and opened the door to one place she never thought she'd go. Campaign HQ was not what she expected. They'd taken over an old storefront and filled it with nondescript desks and tables. A few had computers, but all had phones. There was a distinct red, white and blue theme in the minimalist decor, and every wall was covered in Marshall For Senate signs. It was only a little after nine, but a dozen or so people were already manning phones and stuffing envelopes, and there was a healthy buzz of energy and noise.

Brady was easy to find, standing off to one side and talking on the phone. Margo's eye-candy comment sprang to mind. *Indeed.* The jacket to his suit was draped over a chair behind him, and his shirtsleeves were rolled up over his forearms. They were tanned to the same hue as his face, meaning he didn't always wear long sleeves. Granted, she was hardly an expert on Brady's wardrobe, but it was hard to picture him in anything *other* than a suit and tie.

That was a lie. Frankly it was rather disturbing how easily she could picture Brady in substantially less. Dear Lord, she'd had her hand on the man's *thigh*; between the breadth of his shoulders—which was evident to all, even in a suit—and the firsthand knowledge she now had of his quadriceps, it was quite easy to extrapolate to an appreciation of what Brady was like under that D.C. politico uniform…*ahem*.

She snapped her attention back to his tie. Today, it was a different shade of red with small blue stripes. She had no business noticing anything else.

Remember that.

Even if she didn't already know Brady was the man in charge, simply the way he filled the space and the way the activity buzzed *around* him made it obvious he was the boss.

Then Brady looked up and noticed her. A strange jolt of adrenaline shot through her veins, a combination of excitement and nerves and Brady's presence. He waved her over, but she kept her steps slow and even in the hopes her pulse would calm down before she had to get too close.

A crease formed between Brady's eyes as he ran his eyes over her, but he never paused in his conversation— something about small donors—and Aspyn shifted uncomfortably under his stare. The crisp, distant tone to his voice didn't help, either. When he hung up the phone, one eyebrow went up as he asked, "Who died?"

That rankled her. "Good morning to you, too."

Brady accepted the censure with an amused nod. "Good morning, Aspyn. Good to see you. Seriously, did someone die?"

"What?"

"You look like you're on your way to a funeral. At a convent." Irritation and disapproval colored the statement in equal amounts.

Her outfit felt strange enough as it was. *That* remark didn't help at all. "I figured if I was going to be part of your staff, I should try to look more conservative. More mainstream, less counterculture."

A woman, not too much older than Aspyn, appeared at Brady's elbow and handed him a piece of paper. Brady looked at it, then made introductions. "Aspyn, this is my assistant, Lauren. She'll help you get set up and your phone and email sorted out. Anything you need, let her know."

Lauren seemed friendly enough—and very casually dressed in khakis and a cute sweater. Now she felt slightly overdressed as well as uncomfortable. Brady and Lauren exchanged a look that Aspyn didn't understand, and a second later, Lauren was gone.

Brady immediately went back to business. "Did you prepare a statement like I asked?"

Focus. It's a job, not a fashion show. "I did. Very brief, just how pleased I am that Senator Marshall recognizes the importance of his constituents' concerns and how much I'm looking forward to listening to them and acting as a bridge…" She trailed off as someone else brought Brady something to sign.

"And?" Brady prompted, not looking up.

She had to search for her train of thought. "Um, yeah, acting as a bridge…" This time, it was Brady's phone that caught his attention as a text came in. "Maybe I should see if Kirby has another set of handcuffs," she mumbled.

"Bite your tongue."

So he was listening. "Do you know how hard it is to talk to you when you're doing other things?"

There was that look again, the one that made her feel like he found her oddly amusing—but not in a good way. "I'm a very busy man, Aspyn, and perfectly capable of doing more than one thing at a time."

She nearly took a step back at his tone. This was a different man than the one she'd talked to in an interrogation room and in her apartment. This was worse than the man she'd locked herself in the elevator with. "If everyone in D.C. is like you, no wonder the whole country is frustrated and angry. In order to really listen to people, you have to give them your full attention."

She could swear Brady's jaw tightened, but his mouth curved into a smile that belied the sarcasm in his voice. "Then by all means, let me stop everything and give you my full attention. I'm sure the Majority Whip won't mind if I ignore his text."

"You get by on your looks a lot, don't you?" she snapped.

His eyes widened. "Excuse me?"

He was giving her the chance to walk back that comment. She should take it. The flare of bravado sputtered, and she felt petty and juvenile for resorting to snark. "Nothing." *No sense in getting fired for insubordination on the first day.*

"All right then. This should be quick and painless. I'll go up first, state how this situation has really opened our eyes to the concerns of the citizens and how pleased we are to welcome you to the staff." Brady was still multi-tasking as he spoke, and her irritation was slowly giving a little ground to being impressed with that ability. But only a little. "You'll have a couple of minutes to say your piece, then I'll tell everyone how to contact you, we'll answer questions and be done."

"Okay." She was struggling to process everything. This was obviously business-as-usual to Brady, but she felt four steps behind in her understanding. Hopefully campaigns were a learned skill, and she'd be able to adapt quickly to the mind-set. "And then what?"

Oddly that question got his full attention. "What do you mean?"

"What happens after that?"

Brady looked at her like she wasn't all there. "You listen to people, of course."

"Well, yes…but…" She'd forgotten how hard it was to concentrate when she had his undivided attention. Maybe she should encourage him to answer that text. "But where? Where do I sit? Who do I report to? What else will I be doing?"

For someone who seemed to be so on top of things, a set of what she considered relatively simple questions had him blinking at her.

"You can actually work from home. You don't have to come in here every day."

"But wouldn't that defeat the purpose? How can I make recommendations to the campaign if I don't know what's going on with the campaign?"

Brady rubbed a hand over his forehead. "Then pick one of those desks in the middle. They're for whoever needs them at the moment."

"And?" Getting the simplest of information was like pulling teeth.

"And, what?" Now he sounded exasperated.

"Who do I report to?"

"You don't 'report' to anyone," Brady snapped. He quickly caught himself, though, and his tone became completely professional again. "However, you'll send your comments and recommendations directly to me. How about…let's see…twice a week? I'll forward them to the right staffer."

Okay. Since the moment Brady offered her the job, there'd been a nagging feeling that something wasn't quite right. She'd chalked it up to her own mind playing games, but it grew stronger in the wake of Brady's vagueness. A senatorial campaign had to be a tightly run ship, and Brady seemed like a tightly wound captain who would know every last detail.

Aspyn berated herself for negative thinking. Brady had only slightly more time than she'd had to adjust to the addition of this position. His tightly run ship needed time to adjust course. As far as she could tell, no other campaign had a position like this, so there weren't a lot of preset rules or traditions to fall back on. Maybe once they all saw how this was actually going to go, they'd readjust accordingly. "Okay, then."

Lauren reappeared, this time carrying a pink shirt. "This is for you."

"Why? What's wrong with what I'm wearing?" Black knee-length skirt, black cotton sweater, simple pearl necklace borrowed from Margo's sister, sensible black pumps… If she looked any more respectable and grown-up and mainstream she'd have to drive a minivan and join a country club.

"I wasn't kidding. You look like you're going to a funeral," Brady said as he picked up his jacket and shrugged into it.

"And you don't?" she muttered, drawing raised eyebrows from both Brady and Lauren.

In a tone that almost tripped into condescending, Lauren said, "We're going for a more vibrant and upbeat tone. Something positive to underscore how exciting this is for the campaign."

"I thought I had the whole 'Audrey Hepburn' vibe working for me." Margo had declared the look "chic" last night.

Lauren shook her head. "Fluorescent lighting is unforgiving. With your coloring, that vibe will be 'death-warmed-over' on camera."

"But pink?" She hated pink.

"Pink's a good color for TV. Trust me."

Aspyn looked at Brady, who nodded. "Lauren knows what she's talking about. As soon as you change, we'll get this over with."

Not "Do you mind changing?" or anything remotely like it. Brady was the boss, and he wanted her to change, so he assumed she'd change. *Fine.* She took the shirt from Lauren, who pointed her in the direction of the ladies' room. "I'll be back in a minute." She stopped, gave him the same up-and-down twice-over he'd given her and plastered a smile on her face. "Nice tie, by the way."

Brady's eyes narrowed momentarily, as if he didn't fully trust the compliment. Then he nodded. "Thank you."

"I'm not getting an 'undertaker' vibe at all. Really."

It was a juvenile jab, but it made her feel a little better as she walked off.

* * *

"That went really well. Good job, Aspyn." She looked up in surprise and gave him a smile that spoke of relief.

"Thanks." Aspyn closed the lid of the laptop and turned her chair to face him, adjusting the foot she had tucked under her. After the last reporter left, she'd given back the pink shirt, ditched the pearls and changed from the old-lady shoes into her Birkenstocks. It was a strange look. "It was a bit more nerve-racking than I expected. At least I kept my feet out of my mouth."

He'd meant to offer the compliment quickly and move on, but he found himself perching a hip on the desk instead. "You're a natural in front of the camera. Articulate and clear without being too distant, and sincere without crossing over into smarmy or over-the-top. It's a hard balance to hit, and you did it well."

The praise brought a smile to Aspyn's face. "Wow. Yay me." She pointed to the computer. "I'm already getting email, and someone in the senator's office is forwarding some older messages. It's going to take me a while just to go through it all. But I'm starting to get oddly excited about it."

"Good. Glad to hear it." That was very true. The tide had been turned; the crisis averted. Mission accomplished. Senator Marshall was now being touted as an innovative, responsive public servant and cited as an example for other politicians to emulate. He'd check the poll numbers in a few days, but he didn't doubt they'd see a climb of at least a point or two from this.

So why was he still here talking to Aspyn instead of moving on to one of the many other fires that needed putting out?

Because my ego is enjoying it. He was good at reading people, weighing what their faces and body language said against the words coming out of their mouths. It was a carefully honed skill he prided himself on. Aspyn, however, was especially easy for him to read. Her personality was simply open and friendly, without artifice. It would work well for her in her new "position," as that open and honest demeanor made her seem like someone you could tell your problems to.

But for someone who was constantly watching for subtle clues, Aspyn's thoughts on one topic were blindingly clear.

Aspyn thought he was hot. Not just attractive. Hot. Smokin', actually.

He was a realist when it came to women. He'd been flirted with and hit on by women from all walks of life and every rung of the social ladder since he hit puberty. He was rich, powerfully connected and genetically lucky. The first two were all he really needed in this town; good DNA was just a bonus.

But Aspyn's appreciation was more elemental, and that cut deep into his psyche and libido. She was less-than-impressed with the outside trappings of being Brady Marshall—if anything, she found it annoying—and much more interested in the man underneath. That fact was written on her face.

But she wasn't flirting with him at all, either, which might be part of the appeal. If she'd been flirting, he'd be more wary and likely to keep his distance until her motives became clear. He wasn't a fool. Aspyn was…unique. In many ways.

"Why so smug?" Aspyn laughed. "You totally have a cat-that-ate-the-canary look on your face. I can practically see the feathers hanging out of your mouth. What am I missing?"

"Nothing." Her look called him a liar, but there was no way he could go with the truth. "One of Mack Taylor's staffers called a few minutes ago, completely outraged that we'd pulled you into our camp before they could get hold of you."

"Well, that's interesting. I didn't realize it was some sort of competition."

"Of course it's a competition. Politics is a brutal, full-contact sport. He who hesitates is lost." The joy at out-witting the Taylor campaign *was* slightly marred by the nagging knowledge that while he hadn't done anything technically unethical, he wasn't standing firmly on moral high ground, either. "You've got a lot to learn, Aspyn. Granted, bringing you on board was damage control, but if you look at the bigger picture, having you here is a good thing on many levels."

"I'm glad. On a personal level—mine—you were certainly right about how the press would react. You really know what you're doing. Your dad's lucky to have you on his team."

If she only knew. "It's the family business. It's what the Marshalls do."

The tiniest of clouds crossed Aspyn's face. "And do you like that?"

"Politics? Not always, but campaigns? Yes."

"I meant having a name that's supposed to define you."

Either Aspyn was terribly astute or she had no idea how close to the bone that cut. He chose to believe the latter. His shrug was intentionally casual. "It's just a name."

"And 'a rose by any other name still smells as sweet'?"

"Or stinks, if you're in politics."

She smiled, but he could tell she wasn't entirely convinced. "But your whole family is involved in politics.

What if you decided you didn't like politics and wanted to do something else?"

Aspyn was the first person to ever ask him that. "It's a family business, but not *that* kind of family business. We're not the mafia."

"But you *are* in the family business."

"I could say the same about you." At the question on her face, he clarified, "You're following in your parents' footsteps, too."

She shrugged as well, but her mouth twisted a bit. "It's all I know. It's how I was raised *and* what I was raised to believe."

He nodded in understanding. "It's hard to escape when it's all you know and everyone just assumes…" He hadn't meant to say that, but the look on Aspyn's face made the confession worthwhile. "Maybe I have a bit of 'true believer' in me, as well."

"I'm glad. You should follow your passion."

He could wish Aspyn had phrased that differently. "Passion" took him right back to ideas he had no business entertaining.

His phone started to vibrate, a reminder he was supposed to be running a campaign, not chatting up a staffer. When the ring tone kicked in a second later, it drew a strong line under their conversation *and* the responsibilities of being a Marshall. *Saved by the bell.* "That's my grandmother. I can ignore the Majority Whip…"

She grinned and nodded. "But not your grandmother. I fully understand." Aspyn turned back to her computer as he answered his phone and walked away.

Aspyn stared at her screen without really seeing it. Brady was definitely a puzzle. He could be so formal and stiff—just another politico—and she'd been treated to the full effect of that at this morning's press conference. But that was only one facet of his personality; the conversation they'd just had proved that. There was more to Brady Marshall than he presented to the wide world.

He could certainly turn on the charm or become the guy-next-door. Part of her distrusted *that* facet—if for no other reason than it seemed a political necessity—but she wanted to believe it at the same time, because of moments like the one they'd just shared.

She couldn't quite figure out if she *liked* him or not, and that was a first. Usually she got a feeling about people— good or bad—to go on. Brady's ability to run hot and cold, from frustratingly arrogant to utterly charming, kept her from getting a solid grip of what she thought. Whatever made him tick, it was different than what made other people tick. She was certainly intrigued by him—and oh, *mercy*, she could happily stare at him all day long—but she couldn't figure him out, and that bothered her.

Maybe the fact she *did* like looking at him was what had her feeling off balance. If anyone had ever told her that her hormones would get up and dance over someone like Brady Marshall, she'd have laughed them out of the room. She wasn't a coat-and-tie type of girl. She liked her men to be idealistic, revolutionary and passionate. She liked the outdoorsy type—men who hiked trails and went days without shaving, not because they wanted to conquer the outdoors, but because they wanted to understand and be part of nature.

She stole a glance over her shoulder. Brady hit maybe one of her criteria; he was passionate. Of course, not about the same things she was passionate about… It was ridiculous, really. Even more ridiculous was the strange kick she was getting from that side-show-oddity look he kept giving her. He couldn't figure *her* out, either.

She jumped when a box landed on her desk with a *thump*. Lauren slid it toward her. "This is some of the snail mail they've been receiving at the senator's office that falls outside the usual. You might want to go through it."

"Will do." She pulled the box closer.

"And let me save you some grief. Don't go there."

"The mail?"

"No, I'm talking about Brady. Trust me when I tell you that there's nothing down that path but madness and disappointment."

Oh, dear. Aspyn tried to sound properly casual. "What makes you think…?"

"I've worked for Brady for over three years now, and I've seen it over and over again. Every woman who gets near him develops an adolescent crush on him."

She wasn't surprised. "Except you, obviously."

Lauren laughed. "I didn't say that. I just like my job more." She grew serious and leveled a look at Aspyn. "Brady doesn't get personally involved with staff. Ever. Even if you *were* his type, he wouldn't get involved."

Aspyn felt her jaw drop. It was one thing to be warned about office behaviors, but now she was some kind of "type." The wrong type, it seemed.

Lauren gentled the slap. "I'm not trying to offend you, because honestly, it doesn't matter who or what you are. Brady doesn't fish in the company pond. Even if he were to be tempted, it would be strictly catch and release. Aside from the obvious problems in the scenario, surely you understand that the kind of woman Brady needs in the long run isn't swimming around in here."

While part of her was taking all kinds of offence to Lauren's matter-of-fact statements, part of Aspyn knew the other woman was right. Brady was the de facto heir to the Marshall political legacy, and those blue-blooded power-and-money types stayed in their own circles. *And he's not your type, either, remember?* "I appreciate your candor, but since I object to fishing for sport or profit, it's really unlikely to be a problem."

"Good. You did great with that press conference. You're quick on your feet and you put out a 'trust me' vibe that's totally believable." Aspyn wondered how a "trust me vibe" could be anything but, but she didn't interrupt Lauren to ask. "Play your cards right, absorb all the knowledge you can and you just might find yourself entertaining several job offers after this election. Don't screw that up."

She wouldn't be able to take much more of this before she did start taking offence. "Then I'd better get to work." Aspyn reached for the box of mail, ending the conversation, and Lauren went back to supervising the volunteers manning the phones.

How strange that everyone—okay, a few people— seemed to think a few weeks with the Marshall campaign would put her on a different career path. Or any career path. Much less one in politics.

That was the most ridiculous thing she'd ever heard.

She was meant to be an agent of change, not just another cog in the establishment's machine. But it was her first day on the job and, personal pep talks aside, she still worried she was selling out somehow. Especially if people thought she was heading for a career change. Had she been fooling herself, letting Brady's charm convince her there was merit in this? Buying a bill of goods because she liked the look of the man selling it?

She rubbed her hands across her face. She wasn't a sell-out. She hadn't lost her moral compass or betrayed her beliefs. Even her parents recognized there were many ways to effect change—she didn't always have to be locked to the outside of the gate. Maybe this was how *she* was supposed to do it. Get in on the ground floor and shake things up as she went along. And it wasn't like she'd sold her soul; the minute she didn't like what was happening here, she could leave.

The scary thing, though, was that she kind of liked it here already. And that felt really wrong.

CHAPTER FOUR

ASPYN'S life got quite crowded quite quickly. She spent Friday in a blur, meeting the rest of the staff and volunteers, fielding a few last calls from the press and getting a crash course in Campaigning 101. In some ways, she was more prepared for the job than she'd thought—after all, she'd worked with volunteers or been a volunteer her entire life. *That* part she understood better than some of the salaried staff, and she may have ruffled a few feathers accidentally. It had been both an eye-opening and exhausting day, but there was no rest for the campaign staff, and that now included her.

Except for a couple of hours relieving Margo in the bookstore on Saturday and a very uncomfortable hour spent with Jackie explaining why her association with the People's Planet Initiative had to be severed while she worked for the campaign, Aspyn's weekend was spent wading through emails and voice mails and getting up to speed with Senator Marshall's official positions on the issues. By Sunday night, she was fighting off information overload with chocolate and happy, cheesy disco music. No one could be stressed or depressed or overwhelmed while shakin' their groove thing.

When the phone rang, she muted the music and flopped to the futon as she answered.

"You sound out of breath, Aspyn."

The voice sent adrenaline shooting through her. She'd had little contact with Brady since Lauren's "helpful" advice lecture on Thursday. He had been in the same building Friday afternoon, but he'd been Boss-Man Brady the whole time and the gulf had been rather uncrossable. There hadn't been a repeat of the easy conversation they'd had Thursday. A phone call certainly seemed unusual, though…

Oh, grow up.

She was glad she'd muted the music. "I was um…exercising. A little cardio—" She could tell she was about to babble and put a stop to it. "What's up?"

Well, that wasn't much better. So much for being a professional.

Thankfully Brady didn't comment. "Can you go to Richmond with me in the morning?"

She enjoyed the little skip to her pulse before focusing on the question. *It's just business.* "I guess I can. For what?"

"There's a breakfast with a civic group in the morning. The senator was supposed to attend, but he can't now. I'm going instead."

"Can I ask why you always call him 'the senator' instead of 'my father'?" The inappropriate question was out of her mouth before she could stop it.

"Because he is the senator and in this campaign, he's my boss, not my father."

"He can't be both at the same time?"

"It's not effective. Some distance is preferable in a professional setting."

Okay, so that was a hint. "That makes sense, I guess."

"So, back to the actual purpose of my call…"

"Right. Sorry. Is it normal for you to fill in for the senator when he can't attend something?"

Brady's sigh told her she was doing it again, but he answered nonetheless. "Not exactly. I'm in the bloodline, and therefore the next best thing when the senator can't make it. I thought taking you might be a good idea since you've been such a popular media figure lately." He laughed, but there was something off about it. "And the organizer specifically asked about you. He said he was impressed with how quickly we'd realized what a boon you'd be to our campaign."

"Really? Wow." A bit of pride swelled in her chest.

"It also helps that this group is ninety percent old men and, according to the organizer, you're a sweet young thing."

"Ew." The blatant sexism in that remark bothered her.

"Aspyn, this is a very important group, and we need their support. If showing up with a pretty woman at my side will help gain that, then that's what I'm going to do. Such is the nature of politics—we work every angle we can."

Aspyn knew she should be really disturbed by this. Maybe even righteously indignant, but as Brady said, that was just the way politics worked. But, much to her shame, she was sort of stuck on the "pretty woman" statement. As far as compliments went, it wasn't *that* big a deal, but Aspyn didn't care. Brady said she was pretty.

Since no one could see her, Aspyn didn't worry about the foolish grin that stretched her cheeks. It didn't matter what Lauren said. Actually it did matter, because now that she knew not to read too much into anything, she was perfectly safe to enjoy this moment.

"Okay, then. I'll go. I've been looking over everything Lauren gave me Friday, so I should be mostly up to speed on the likely questions or issues they might bring up."

"Good. We can also use the drive to be sure you're prepped well. I'll pick you up at five."

"In the morning?" *Ugh.*

"Breakfast meetings are normally held in the mornings." That look Brady gave her when she prodded him obviously had a tonal equivalent. She couldn't see his face, but she knew what it would look like.

Still... "Brunch seems like it would be far more civilized."

"Welcome to the real world."

What did he mean by that? "I was kidding." *Sort of, but he didn't know that.*

"I'll see you at five. Good night."

It wasn't until later that night, as she was eyeballing her wardrobe critically in search of something suitable for a breakfast meeting, that the full force of what she'd agreed to hit her.

First, she was actually going out as a face for the Marshall campaign. Wow. That wasn't part of her job description. And though he had said her presence was requested by the organizer, surely Brady wouldn't let her represent the campaign if he didn't trust her to represent it well. She'd only just started this job, but she knew this was a big deal—and not something that newbies normally did. She should be pleased—proud, even—that Brady wanted her to go to Richmond with him.

With him. Belated realization nearly forced her to sit down. Richmond was a two-hour drive from here. That equaled four hours in a car with Brady. Four hours of close confines with a man who made her heart beat dangerously fast. Four hours with a man she was majorly attracted to who never got involved with his staff.

Especially, as Lauren had stressed, someone like *her*.

Oh, she could handle it. She was perfectly capable of knowing where lines had to be drawn and then staying on the right side of those lines. It wasn't like she couldn't be trusted not to throw herself in the man's lap in some kind of lustful frenzy.

But that didn't mean she wouldn't spend four hours *wanting* to.

The limo pulled to a stop in front of the bookstore where Aspyn waited out front in the predawn gloom hugging something to her chest. The driver opened the door and assisted Aspyn in before passing her the largest coffee mug Brady had ever seen. As she took it with a grateful smile, Brady realized that was what she'd been hugging. It was practically a coffee urn.

"Morning," she mumbled as she got settled. Her curls were still slightly damp from the shower, and she drank from her enormous cup almost desperately. Aspyn obviously wasn't a morning person.

When she leaned back, eyes closed, he chuckled. "Well, aren't you a ray of sunshine?"

Her brows drew together like she was in pain, but her eyes didn't open. "It's five o'clock in the morning. There are no rays of sunshine anywhere." She sighed and kicked her shoes off as the limo eased away from the curb. "God doesn't even get up this early."

Aspyn's grumblings would be amusing—maybe even cute—except that she turned sideways in the other seat and lifted her feet as she got comfortable. As she did, her skirt twisted and slid up, giving him a clear view of shapely calves and lean thighs. With her sleepy features and half smile, Aspyn looked like she belonged in a bed, tangled in warm covers and tempting a lover back for an early morning kiss. Or more.

He reached for his own coffee, glad Aspyn's eyes were still closed. He doubted she was even aware of the erotic picture she created—much less creating it intentionally—but that didn't damp the zing of electricity that hit him like he'd been Tasered.

Maybe taking Aspyn to Richmond wasn't such a good idea, after all. Although she wasn't currently giving him that "tasty treat" look, the earthy, artless sensuality of her drew him like a magnet. *That* was new for him. He'd always been with women who were polished and sophisticated, but in comparison to Aspyn, that polish now seemed plastic and fake.

Aspyn seemed comfortable in her own skin, sure and unapologetic about who she was. That lack of artifice was more alluring than Brady expected. He'd been in the political machine so long that he was far more used to games, hidden agendas, power plays and the assumption everyone wanted something. Aspyn was just Aspyn. What you saw was what you got.

Why *that* was suddenly important to his libido defied explanation. But it was.

He dragged his eyes away from the long line of her legs and back to the computer on his lap. Aspyn wasn't a typical employee, but she was still off-limits for a laundry list of reasons. They came from different worlds, had different expectations. It was far safer to limit himself to women who understood *his* world and rules that governed it. He didn't need drama—didn't *want* drama—in his personal life, and certainly not the kind of drama that could come from his personal life becoming public fodder.

Plus, the election was where he needed to focus. The last thing he needed right now was distractions. Especially Aspyn-like distractions.

Opening her eyes, Aspyn extended her legs, ruining the view as she asked, "Are you naturally a morning person or are you just better at pretending?" She took a large sip of the coffee, then held the cup under her chin and breathed in the steam.

"Probably not by the standard definition, but I can function in the mornings with only a minimum of caffeine."

"I'll be fully functional in a few more minutes." She tugged at her skirt. Sitting up a little more, she shrugged off the wrap covering her shoulders and spread her arms. "I tried for 'conservative-but-less-funeral-like' today. Hope this is acceptable for a breakfast meeting."

For Aspyn, the colorful and flowing skirt probably did qualify as "conservative." Her jewelry was understated— nothing jangling this morning—and the shoes on the floor were simple black flats. It wasn't what he'd normally expect from a campaign employee, but it worked for her. Probably only because it was Aspyn. He couldn't picture her in a pantsuit. "It's fine."

"Good." She blew out her breath. "I didn't even think about wardrobe when I took this job, and now it's all happening so fast, I can't quite keep up."

"That's understandable. It has been a crazy few days. I'm impressed you're doing as well as you are."

An eyebrow went up. "Actually you sound surprised, not impressed."

Aspyn didn't play games. He liked that. "How about I'm surprised that I'm impressed. It takes a lot to do either."

"How very sad." She settled back into the corner again and cuddled her coffee. She seemed serious.

"Excuse me?"

"That's a very bleak outlook to have. It's a good thing you're *almost* a morning person."

He shouldn't ask—and really didn't want to—but he couldn't help himself. "Because?"

"Because I don't know how else you'd manage to drag yourself out of bed every day when you think there's nothing waiting to surprise you. Where's your optimism? Your joie de vivre?"

He snorted without meaning to. The system had beaten both out of him years ago. "You seem to have enough for both of us."

"Joie de vivre?"

"And optimism."

She cut her eyes at him over her coffee mug in challenge. "And again, you say that like it's a bad thing."

"Too much optimism makes it difficult to deal with reality. And I deal in reality."

She nodded. "True. But you're not a true pessimist, either. If you were, you'd constantly be surprised when things went well."

Once again, she made him laugh. "You do have a point."

"I know." She grinned. "And I'm glad you finally see it. I'm supposed to help people become more aware, you know."

That was the oddest thing he'd ever heard. "What?"

"For the Druids, aspen trees were believed to help facilitate awareness and transition."

Okay, that was a bit of a non sequitur. Even more confusing, she'd said it like it was supposed to mean something. "And you believe that has…what to do with you, exactly?"

She sat up a little straighter. "My parents believe that people can make a difference. They named me Aspyn in the hopes that I would channel the power of the aspen tree and be a transformative force in the world."

No, that *was the oddest thing he'd ever heard.*

She met his eyes. "My bigger purpose in this world is to somehow help bring awareness and focus and help find opportunities for positive change."

Aspyn's voice lacked any humor or sarcasm. She actually seemed to believe what she was saying. "That's a lot to put on a kid."

"Well, my parents are optimists, too. And, hey, what do you know, I'm kind of doing that. Granted, it's probably not quite how my parents imagined it, but it's still a chance to make a difference."

Some things about Aspyn were starting to make sense, and guilt twinged him about the reality of the situation. He should probably reel her in before she got too excited. "Aspyn, you might want to temper your expectations a bit."

She waved a hand in response. "Don't worry. I'm an optimist, but I know there are limitations and realities of what I can do. But that doesn't mean I'm not always on the lookout for possibilities."

Time to change the subject before she started looking for specifics in those possibilities. "Caffeine really does make a difference for you, doesn't it? Instant human."

"Yeah. It's a weakness, I know, but I'm addicted." She seemed to think for a moment, growing more serious, then she swung her legs around to face him and leaned forward with her elbows on her knees. She had a tiny, forced smile that put him on guard for what was about to come. "That brings up something—"

She stopped as the limo slowed, and looked out the window in confusion as they came to a stop. A moment later, the door opened and Lauren climbed in, taking the seat next to Aspyn.

"Morning, Brady. Hi, Aspyn. I brought bagels."

Aspyn looked a little confused as she took the bag Lauren handed her.

He might regret this, but he was discovering he was a glutton for punishment. "What were you saying, Aspyn?"

"Nothing important. Thanks for the bagel, Lauren."

Lauren, with her usual unwavering focus, jumped right in to the schedule for the day. The friendly, comfortable atmosphere evaporated as Lauren's crisp efficiency filled the air instead. For the first time, he rather resented that feeling.

"Since we'll be there anyway, I've set up a couple of meetings. I've set up a meet-and-greet for you, too, Aspyn." A small snide smile crossed Lauren's face. "A chance for you to do some listening in-person."

Aspyn stiffened slightly and nodded. He was aware of Lauren's displeasure with the addition of Aspyn to the staff; he'd already had an earful about how she found it redundant and rather insulting as it implied the staffs of the senator's office and campaign weren't doing their jobs properly. While she claimed to understand the PR motives behind it, it still rubbed Lauren the wrong way. He hadn't known Aspyn was aware of Lauren's feelings. Great. The *last* thing he needed was turf-wars or catfights within the campaign.

Aspyn stayed mostly quiet as they headed south, only asking the occasional question, but taking copious notes the entire time—about what, he wasn't entirely sure. Lauren directed the entire conversation at him, anyway, as she jumped from topic to topic without any superfluous digressions to anything that wasn't directly campaign-related. It was completely normal, but it bothered him today.

And though he probably wouldn't have liked the question, he never did get a chance to ask Aspyn what she'd wanted to say. And that bothered him, too.

I am a world-class idiot. What other explanation did she have for her behavior? Of course Brady's assistant would accompany him to Richmond. *Duh.* This was a business trip, not some kind of date. Although she'd been nervous about spending that much quality time with Brady, it wasn't until Lauren got in the limo that she realized she'd been looking *forward* to it.

Lauren's warning replayed in her head. Maybe she should have paid a little more attention. She should definitely rethink her idea she could flirt around the edges of a Brady Marshall crush without flirting with disaster. She might not be setting herself up for the heartbreak Lauren mentioned, but she could definitely get her feelings hurt.

It also didn't help that Brady was practically Jekyll and Hyde. Dr.-Jekyll-Brady was fun, approachable, interesting, and devastating to her higher brain functions. Mr.-Hyde-Brady was aloof and untouchable, and every inch a stuffed-shirt, political bureaucrat who made her want to smack him if she weren't still half-cowed by that part of him. And he could move between the two personalities in a blink. She'd been enjoying herself this morning with Dr.-Jekyll-Brady until Lauren showed up and changed him into Mr.-Hyde-Brady like an evil fairy godmother.

But which one was he really? She normally trusted her

instincts, but Brady had her so confused she didn't know what to believe. She wanted to believe that the stuffed shirt was all a front, but she'd met enough snake oil salesmen to not trust charm and friendliness blindly.

And if Brady wanted to sell snake oil, he'd be a master. The speculations that Brady would follow his father and grandfather into politics had a firm foundation. Watching him work the crowd after breakfast, she realized he could be both Jekyll and Hyde at the same time: uptight enough to make the people feel like he was competent and trustworthy, yet friendly enough that people liked him anyway. It was impressive yet off-putting at the same time.

Plus, she was so far out of her league with this job it wasn't even funny. She had two pages of notes just from listening to Brady and Lauren this morning. There was so much she didn't understand that she'd need to do research just to be able to ask a sensible question. What little understanding she had of this whole political thing would rattle around inside a peanut shell. But it was all so fascinating, if a little disillusioning, and she really wanted to learn.

And Brady? Well, he was certainly fascinating and confusing. Disillusioning? That was still to figure out. Sadly she doubted research would help her any with that problem.

It was time to grow up, to look at the big picture and decide how to make the most of this. Brady was a hottie, but he was off-limits and any mooning at all over him would only distract her from what she could do with this opportunity. The thought she couldn't handle a professional relationship with a man because she was attracted to him made her sound immature and foolish. She was better than that. She wasn't going to squander this opportunity over something like sex.

Last week, Brady had called her passionate and sincere. But passion and sincerity wouldn't get her anywhere unless she could be professional as well. She needed to focus.

On something other than Brady Marshall.

Aspyn remained rather quiet the rest of the day, and Brady almost found himself missing her conversation. Aspyn had a way of drawing people—including him to his surprise—out by just talking to them until they had no choice but to talk back. And then she listened. Plus, Aspyn was pretty much the only person around—other than his brothers—who didn't always want to talk about campaign strategies, poll numbers, or fund-raising. It was a nice distraction from the usual.

Even worse, something had gone out of her eyes. The focus was still there, and she listened to all the conversations intensely, but with less excitement.

To top it off, Aspyn no longer seemed to watch him with that purely physical appreciation he'd let stroke his ego. He didn't know he was shallow enough to care about such a thing, so *that* was a new and disturbing revelation for him, but it bothered the hell out of him nevertheless.

His normal approach to problem solving was head-on, straight to the point, but this situation…? Brady wasn't even sure what the point *was*, much less how to approach it. It didn't help, either, that the problem kept niggling at him, distracting him from what he needed to be doing.

And since it wasn't something he could really bring up in front of Lauren, by the time they arrived back in Arlington, Brady wasn't really fit company for anyone.

Back at HQ, Aspyn tried to blend into the crowd—as much as she could blend anywhere. She stuck out, even when she wasn't outlandishly dressed, simply by her personality. The ink was barely dry on her contract, and she was already giving several of the other staffers fits. Within an hour, his volunteer coordinator pulled him aside in wounded outrage after Aspyn provided her two cents on organizing the teams for the door-to-door canvass and was backed by the volunteers against the original plan.

No sooner than he had *that* sorted out when his media director informed him that if Aspyn didn't stop with her litany of complaints about the number of trees "murdered" for the production of campaign literature, real murder might occur. When the press secretary headed his way, steam coming out of his ears, Brady wondered if it were really possible for a campaign to implode due to one staff member.

And Aspyn seemed unaware of the trouble she caused. She was currently in a huddle with three of the field agents, and Brady figured they'd be making their way to his office soon enough.

Coupled with the fact Aspyn was doing an excellent job annoying him simply by pretending he didn't exist now, Brady wasn't getting a damn thing done. She'd undergone a huge attitude change since this morning and he didn't know why. *Why* it annoyed him so much didn't stand up to logic or reason, but that didn't lessen the feeling any. *That* annoyed him even more.

All in all, Aspyn was thoroughly messing with his head, derailing his attempts to get things done, and making him question—*again*—the wisdom of bringing her on staff.

Then, as if she knew she was the focus of his thoughts, Aspyn looked up from her huddle over one of the computers and gave him a half smile that *almost* echoed her earlier smiles of "appreciation" before she looked away.

Damn it. That sealed it. Since he couldn't get anything

done with her here—and she showed no signs of going home—he'd leave. He liked to be around; it kept him on top of things and in the loop, but he could stay in the loop via email or phone. He had a good staff; they could certainly handle it for the rest of the day.

Lauren sputtered in disbelief when he told her he was leaving for the day. He saw her surreptitiously double-check his calendar as if looking for a reason why. He couldn't explain logically why he needed to leave, so he didn't provide an answer to her unspoken question. He also knew he should deal with Aspyn now, but he didn't quite trust himself in his current mood. Provided his entire staff didn't quit overnight, he'd sort it all out tomorrow.

Good Lord, he really needed to get a life. The campaign was consuming him. And as much as he hated to admit either of his brothers could be right about anything, both Finn and Ethan had called his attention to it recently. He was working too hard and not playing at all.

Once the election was over—relieving some of the stress—he'd investigate reinvigorating his social life, because that was the only explanation he could come up with to make sense of this whole Aspyn thing. Celibacy and isolation obviously weren't good for him.

Because the only other explanation was that he was losing his mind.

He was out the door and nearly to his car when he heard her calling.

"Brady, wait!"

In a flash of déjà vu, Aspyn caught up to him, matched her pace to his and just started talking. The next step would be handcuffs, and his reaction today would be much different than last time... He forced himself to focus. "What *are* you talking about?"

"The senator. When should I plan to meet with him? Lauren told me to ask you."

"I'm sure he'll come by HQ at some point. You can introduce yourself then."

She rolled her eyes. "Not meet him, Brady. Meet *with* him. I want to be sure I'm really prepared and up to speed on everything before I do. I know I'll need to meet with you first—after you've had a chance to look over the report I'm preparing, of course," she added as they turned the corner of the building into the deserted back parking lot, "but I want—"

He held up a hand. "This is a very busy time. Congress is still in special session and the senator is trying to conduct the country's business *and* campaign to keep his seat. I doubt he'll have that kind of time until after the election." Brady unlocked his door, tossed his briefcase inside, then turned back to face her—leaving the car door open in the hope she'd take the hint. "Sift through everything and write up what you feel is important. Give it to me, and I'll pass it along to the right staffer."

Aspyn ignored his hint, leaning against the car instead and crossing her arms over her chest. "That seems to blatantly contradict everything you've said to the press and everyone else for the last couple of days."

"No." He chose his words carefully. "You are a part of this *campaign*. Your data will be used to help us tailor and target appropriately. However, nothing can happen *in practice* until after the election. That is when the data you collect now will be...useful. There's a big difference between campaigning and actually governing."

Her lips thinned into an irritated line.

"Aspyn, I appreciate your enthusiasm. I really do. So does the senator, but..."

"But what?"

He sighed. "First, you need to focus on your position and let the others do the jobs they were hired for. We work as a team, but they know what they're doing and you don't yet." He waited for her to nod her understanding. "Second, you need to…realize the limitations. There's a bigger picture here. I know you don't see it yet, but that's what I have to concentrate on. Change doesn't happen overnight."

She thought for a moment and nodded. "I see."

It was too much to hope. "Do you really?"

"No, actually, I don't. I was humoring you."

Good Lord. "I wish you wouldn't do that."

"And I wish you wouldn't patronize me. I'm not stupid."

"I never said you were," he tried to interject, but Aspyn kept talking over him.

"I get the feeling you don't like me very much, but I am a part of this campaign now—"

The first part of that statement caught him off guard. "Wait." Surprisingly the flood of words stopped. "What makes you think I don't like you?"

She shrugged. "It's obvious you don't really want me working here."

"Those are two completely different issues."

Aspyn blew out her breath in a noisy sigh. "Well, *that* wasn't exactly the strong denial I was hoping for."

He needed a drink. Now. "Is there a point to this conversation, Aspyn?"

She thought for a moment, then stood up straight and squared her shoulders. "Yes, there is. In just a few days, I've discovered how little I know about politics or how Congress works. I can't work within the system to effect change if I don't understand how the system works. There's so much I need to learn. You said it yourself. And I think you're the right person to teach me."

She'd placed her hand on his arm as she spoke and the combination of her touch and his body's deliberate misinterpretation of what kinds of lessons Aspyn wanted sent his blood rushing south. Every muscle in his body tensed.

Aspyn pulled her hand back like she'd been burned. She paused and the silence stretched out. Finally she asked, "Do you believe in Fate, Brady?"

"No."

"Well, I do." Impatience tinged her words. "And I've been thinking all afternoon that since Fate brought us together, it must want us to accomplish something. Together."

"No, your friend Kirby and his damn handcuffs brought us toge—" He cleared his throat. "Brought all this on."

"But you just said you have to look at the big picture. Can you not imagine me in that picture anywhere?"

At this moment, he could imagine Aspyn just fine. Naked. Head thrown back in pleasure, curls bouncing… He forced the image out of his head and tried to focus on what she was saying.

"You may not like me very much, but I like you. Most of the time," she clarified. "But I think our differences are what make this…situation so unique. The things I think you and I could do together—the things we could learn from each other—don't require that we actually like each other."

Had she been planning this little speech? Intentionally choosing words that his overheated body could warp into something completely inappropriate for their "situation?" Though Aspyn's face was usually so readable, he didn't trust his instincts at the moment to read it properly. But

Aspyn *was* closer to him than really necessary, and her green eyes were wide…

And if he was wrong, the repercussions could be ugly. He should step back, put proper professional distance—both literal and metaphorical—between them. There were plenty of people on his staff who could answer Aspyn's questions, teach her whatever it was she hoped to learn…

But even as his rational brain worked through the *shoulds*, his hands were on her arms, and he was pulling her closer to him. Aspyn rose on her toes to meet him halfway, and her body pressed against his, narrowing his "big picture" to something very, very specific.

Her mouth was soft, her lips parting to receive him, and the heat he found there scorched his soul. There was no hesitancy, no holding back, just the intensity of her desire that swept over him as she took and gave in equal measure. The honesty in her response was a powerful aphrodisiac, making the blood roar in his ears as he lost himself in the fire she sparked.

His hands slid to her waist, anchoring her against him, as her arms twined around his shoulders and tightened to support herself as she melted into him. The kiss grew deeper, taking on a life of its own, hungry and powerful and demanding. Her breasts pressed against his chest, and her hips aligned to his as he slid his hands over her back to her shoulders…

What the hell am I doing?

It took all he had to break the kiss, untangling her arms from his neck, and setting her firmly a safe distance away. He took deep breaths, willing his body back under control, fisting his hands to keep from reaching for her again.

Aspyn blinked in confusion. Her eyes were wide and unfocused, and passion colored her cheeks. Her breaths were uneven and shaky, more proof of desire his body didn't need while he could still taste her. She licked her lips—still moist and swollen—and swallowed hard, sending another slash of fire through him. "Brady? Is something…"

"That shouldn't have happened." He cleared his throat and tugged his coat back into place. "My apologies, Aspyn. It won't happen again."

CHAPTER FIVE

BRADY'S words hit her like a slap across the face. One second he was kissing her like…like…like she was the very air he needed to exist, and now he was *apologizing* for it?

She was still shaking with desire, and he was adjusting his cuffs like nothing had happened. That was the closest she'd ever come to feeling the earth move and Brady was…clearly *un*moved.

Her lips were moving—she could feel them because they were still tingling—but no words were coming out.

Aspyn didn't know exactly when her purpose had shifted—she certainly hadn't chased Brady outside with *this* on her mind—but… *Wow*. Just *wow*. That had been a kiss to top all kisses ever.

At least for her.

She'd been right: the body under that expensive suit was spectacular. She'd had every inch of her body pressed against it and the planes and shapes were seared into her skin. And she now knew that polished, urbane, buttoned-up exterior was partly window dressing; she'd tasted the real Brady underneath that facade—the earthy, primal man at his core—and it had awakened something in her.

And now he was rejecting her.

That sliced deep.

Brady opened his mouth to say something else, but she cut him off.

"Don't apologize." She didn't want to hear it. In fact, it might just kill her to hear it again. "I'll just go back inside now." Her legs weren't quite steady, but they managed to work well enough to get her around the corner and out of Brady's sight before they failed and she had to lean against the building for support.

She'd obviously read that situation all wrong, and that brought everything else she thought she knew about the current state of events into question. She'd talked herself out of a crush just hours ago only to end up kissing him. Which, obviously, was a mistake.

Well, as far as her libido was concerned that kiss was far from a mistake, but she needed to listen to a far more rational part of herself. Her instincts—and her hormones—couldn't be trusted, it seemed.

So much for all that talk about "professional distance." How was she supposed to face him now, much less work for him? The humiliation and confusion made her feel a little sick as they clashed with the residual desire still curling through her.

She took a deep breath and fanned her face. Then she pushed off the wall and straightened her clothes. Brady's car came around the corner and turned in the opposite direction as she opened the door to HQ.

She still believed that Fate had brought her here, but Fate could be cruel sometimes. But since Fate couldn't have given her a more literal sign of "moving on," that's what she should do.

* * *

By Thursday, Aspyn had half-convinced herself The Kiss was just an aberration, no big deal, and that she could just put it out of her mind and move on.

Well, not *totally* out of her mind. That kiss had rocked her world, and her nerves were primed and on full alert. She'd let Margo make her a valerian tisane—and she drank every last drop—to try to take the edge off, but the results weren't exactly as effective as she'd hoped for. Residual desire hummed through her, making her distracted and irritable, and no herbal remedy could counteract the effects of Brady's kiss.

Of course, the one thing that *should* have helped—the total absence of Brady for the last couple of days—wasn't working, either. She didn't necessarily relish the idea of facing him—wasn't sure how she could—but facing him would give her a clue of how things were in his mind and how he expected to go on from here. Well, he'd made it clear what direction things *wouldn't* be going, but would he acknowledge it? Pretend it didn't happen? She needed that line drawn, needed to create the boundary, and she couldn't do that while Brady was off in different parts of the state.

His absence meant she didn't have her footing yet, so instead of being able to concentrate, all it had done was make her jumpy and off-center. The suspense was killing her. And the physical response she couldn't get under control wasn't helping, either.

While the kiss hadn't meant anything to him, *something* she'd said to Brady on Monday must have made an impact, because on Tuesday morning, Matthew—who used to be someone she only barely interacted with—became her new best friend.

He was young, only a couple of years out of college,

but Matthew seemed to know pretty much everything. He had a degree in Political Science with a minor in History. He'd worked as a Congressional Page and later as an intern. He knew everybody and everything and no matter what question Aspyn asked, he seemed to have a ready—and understandable—answer.

Lauren, supposedly, was the one who sent Matthew to tutor her, but Aspyn knew Brady had to be the impetus. It annoyed her on a basic level, but how could she really complain about it? She'd made her case for wanting to learn, and he'd provided a teacher.

Matthew helped her smooth the feathers she'd ruffled and got her back on good terms with the rest of the staff. Then, he set himself to the task of educating her about how things really worked in the system, and Aspyn was getting a better picture of where she'd been going wrong before.

Like the importance of a clear set of defined objectives; the broad spectrum ideals—like she'd been dealing with at PPI—had to be narrowed and focused in order to make people want to listen. And how she needed to think about possible solutions—and ramifications of those solutions—if she wanted people to take her seriously. Matthew was patient as he battered her optimism and idealism with reality, but things were starting to make sense.

Even if she didn't like it much. Like now.

"It's not that simple, Aspyn—"

"It should be. Either we value the First Amendment or we don't."

"But the question of what to do when your rights infringe upon the rights of others can't be ignored, either." The patient, placating tone of his voice irked her. "I promise you, if you send that report as is, you're shooting yourself in the foot."

"The whole purpose of writing this report is to bring these kinds of issues to the senator's attention."

"Senator Marshall is not a magician. In an ideal world, your argument makes sense, but we don't live in an ideal world."

"Duh." She pointed at her computer. "Case in point, right here."

"And I'm telling you, your narrow view isn't going to work."

Shock caused her jaw to drop, but outrage followed quickly enough to close it. "Narrow? My views are *not* narrow. I'm as broad-minded as they come."

Someone called Matthew's name. "Then try to see the bigger picture," Matthew advised, before he went to see what they needed.

Aspyn let the cursor hover over the send button. Attached to the email was her first official report to Brady on the issues considered most important by likely voters— with an addendum on issues she thought were particularly interesting or important, whether or not they had wide support. Matthew may have taken issue with some of it, but she still felt the need to send it as it was. This "bigger picture" argument was really starting to annoy the hell out of her. Half the problems in this country were directly caused by D.C.'s need to weasel everything to death. Rights shouldn't be debatable, yet somehow they were. She took a deep breath as she hit Send. Her optimism wasn't going down without a fight, damn it.

Next on her agenda for the day was the information Matthew had left with her about the bills coming up for a vote soon. She was still behind the curve, but she planned to catch up eventually.

The bell over the door jingled and she looked up as a dark-haired woman came in. Everyone else seemed hunched over phones or in the middle of something, so Aspyn went to greet her. "Hi. Can I help you?"

The woman didn't look like she was from Capitol Hill; jeans and a sweater might fly here at HQ, but definitely not in the city. Plus, her attitude was far too casual. Probably not the press, either. A new volunteer? A constituent? "I'd like to see Brady," the woman said with a bright smile.

Join the club. "Sorry, but he's not here. Can someone else help you?"

She shook her head, causing a long, shiny ponytail to curve over her shoulder. Aspyn had serious hair envy. "No, it's personal business. Not campaign stuff. I'm Lily Black." Lily's smile turned proud and pleased as she held up her left hand to show a very impressive piece of bling. "Soon to be Lily Marshall, though."

"Oh." Aspyn's heart hit her stomach like a rock. *Oh.* "You're Brady's…?" The thought she'd kissed another woman's fiancé, even accidentally…

"Oh, no." Lily made a sound suspiciously like a snort. "No, no, dear God, *no.* There are three Marshall boys— Brady, Ethan and Finn. Ethan's mine."

Of course she knew Brady had brothers. She wanted to smack herself at her overreaction. Although… A fiancée would help explain Brady's strange reaction to that kiss, but the relief flowing through her that he didn't was stronger than her need for an explanation. "Congratulations."

"Thanks. I still can't quite believe it myself." Lily stopped and cocked her head to the side. "Have we met before? Your face seems so familiar for some reason."

"We haven't met, but I'm Aspyn Breedlove. I'm the—"

"Of *course*. You're the new headache. I knew you looked familiar. I'm so pleased to meet you."

She'd been called a lot of things in her life, but *that* was new. "Headache?"

"Campaign headache. It used to be me, but I'm happy to pass the mantle on to you." The shock Aspyn felt must have shown on her face, because Lily wrinkled her nose and put a hand on her arm. "Sorry, I didn't mean to insult you. It's just Brady and the senator were all spun up over me until you came along. They were afraid I'd be a campaign liability—and there was chance for a little while that I might—but then you totally stole the spotlight."

That still didn't make a lot of sense, but… "Accidentally, I assure you."

"Regardless how it happened, I'm indebted to you. The last week or so has been bliss. Well, for *me*," she corrected, "not so much for you, I imagine."

"But it's working out well." The statement came easier than expected and, all things considered, it was still surprisingly true. "I'm very excited to be on staff—however it came to be."

"Good. And good luck." Lily held out a slim envelope. "Could you give Brady this?"

"Sure." *If he ever shows up.*

Lily looked around. "You know, this isn't at all what I expected campaign headquarters to look like."

"You're not involved with the campaign?"

There was that strange laugh again. "Oh, no. Ethan and I stay away from the day-to-day stuff." Lily cocked her head. "You look confused."

"No. Well, I just assumed it was family thing. You know, everyone on the team."

"The Marshalls are a big family. Plenty of people to go around to the various activities. Ethan stays busy on the business side, so we're not much on the campaigning."

"That makes sense." Aspyn was a little disappointed to hear that. Lily was a bit odd and not at all what she'd expect a Marshall fiancée to be, but Aspyn's gut feeling had her kind of liking Lily for some reason. She might be an interesting person to get to know.

"I'm not going to stick around and get in everyone's way. Welcome to the campaign, Aspyn. I hope you enjoy your new position. I can't wait to tell Ethan I met you."

"Really?"

Lily's nod was serious. "Oh, yeah. After what Brady's told him, Ethan's now terribly curious about you."

Brady had been talking to his brother about her? The jolt that went through her defied explanation. "Why? I'm not all that interesting."

"Well, you certainly got Brady's attention in a big way, and that's always fun for his brothers. Ethan and Finn have absolutely loved this. It takes a lot to get Brady spun up."

Spun up, huh? Was this before or after four-thirty Monday afternoon? "Because...?" she prompted.

"Because... Well, I'm sure you know by now that Brady is a bit, um... How to say it nicely...?"

"Tightly wound sometimes?" Aspyn offered.

"I was searching for something regarding the existence of a stick in a certain part of his anatomy, but 'tightly wound' will do."

Aspyn was beginning to rethink her earlier decision to like Lily. "Brady may be a bit 'tightly wound' but he's got a lot of responsibilities with this campaign, so that's completely understandable. And this whole thing with me—not *me*, personally, but the press attention I brought—only added to that. I'll admit I don't know him as well as you do, but I don't think Brady is…" Aspyn trailed off as Lily's eyebrows rose and a small smile began to tug at the corners of her mouth.

"I see."

Damn. She took the envelope from Lily. "I'll give this to Lauren. She'll see that Brady gets it."

"Thank you." Lily was still fighting her smile. "It was very nice meeting you, Aspyn. I hope to see you again."

Not if I crawl into a hole and never come out again. "You, too." Aspyn casually walked back to her desk as Lily left, hoping no one had overheard their conversation.

There was just no end to the ways she could make a fool of herself. It was too much to hope that Lily would forget about their entire meeting—much less not report it back to various Marshall brothers.

Ugh. She was not cut out for politics.

"How's your happy hippie working out?"

When Ethan had appeared at his front door, claiming to need an escape from all things wedding-related, Brady had been grateful for the distraction. He should have known better.

"She's not a hippie, and she's certainly not 'my' anything." The very last thing he wanted to do tonight was discuss Aspyn with his brother. Brady searched through the channels to find the baseball game, then sat back with his beer, hoping Ethan would take the hint.

Ethan took the armchair next to his. "That's not what Lily says."

"No offense to Lily, but I'm not really interested in her opinion of Aspyn."

"Honestly, neither am I, but it's Lily's second-favorite

topic of conversation at the moment. It's only fair you should have to hear it, too."

"Then find her something else to talk about. Current events. Movies. You two should join a book club or something."

Ethan chuckled. "Ah, if it were only that easy. Lily says Aspyn's quite cute—in a wholesome, all-natural, flower-child kind of way."

Brady reached for the remote and turned up the volume. He didn't want to talk about Aspyn since he was working very hard to not even think about her—and specifically the way she felt against his body and under his hands. His body grew hard at the memory. "Can we just watch the game?"

Keeping his eyes on the TV, Ethan casually said, "Lily thinks you're sleeping with her."

"What?" He nearly spilled his drink.

Ethan chuckled as he tipped up his bottle. "You heard me."

He leaned back and closed his eyes. "I hope you're the only one she's sharing that theory with."

Ethan frowned. "So it's true?"

"No." *Damn it.* "I am not sleeping with Aspyn."

"Yet?"

Why didn't my parents just stop after one child? "I'm going to pretend you didn't say that, because I really don't want to have to punch you in the mouth."

"Why not?"

"Because the Grands would kill me for ruining your wedding photos. It might be worth it, though. Maybe I should."

Ethan waved away the threat. "No, why aren't you and Aspyn—"

"Are you seriously asking me why I'm not having sex with a woman I barely know *and* who happens to work for me?"

Ethan shook his head. "Technically you both work for our father."

Like he wasn't already well aware of that fact and try-ing to ignore it. "Shut up."

"Hmm, I seem to have hit a nerve. Interesting."

"No, it's not interesting at all. I just want to have a beer and watch the game without listening to you yammer."

"Fine. We'll watch the game." Ethan relaxed back in his chair and propped his feet on the table. "It is interest-ing, though, you haven't denied that you'd like to have sex with her."

"I'm warning you. It's never too late to prune the fam-ily tree."

"Ah, this grumpiness speaks to the truth. It's not just the campaign making you cranky. Celibacy doesn't agree with you. If you're not interested in Aspyn, why don't you give Isabelle a call? She's made it very clear she'll wel-come you back with open arms."

Do not take the bait. Brady kept his eyes on the TV. "We're a big family, Ethan, and we all look a lot alike. It could take weeks, months even, before anyone really no-ticed you were missing."

"It was just an observation."

"Just observe the game."

From the corner of his eye, he saw Ethan shrug and set-tle back in his chair. *Good.* Now, with Ethan finally—if probably only temporarily—silenced, Brady tried to turn his attention to the game as well. He needed to clear his head, change the direction of his thoughts. But any prog-ress he'd made putting Aspyn out of his mind had been completely undone with a simple "Why not?" from his idiot brother. And bringing up Isabelle… She was beautiful and sophisticated and from a good family, but against Aspyn… Izzy was a diamond and just as cold, but Aspyn was an opal, full of color and fire inside.

Jewels? Oh, dear Lord, he really was losing his mind. *Just think about baseball.*

Yeah, that wasn't working now, either.

One person gets sick and the whole damn place falls apart. It seemed Lauren really was the linchpin holding HQ together, and everyone was scrambling to keep it together while she was out with a case of food poisoning.

"Except for me," Aspyn mumbled, drawing the attention of the taxi driver.

"Did you say something?"

"No." She, as the low person on the totem pole, was the staff member least critical to keeping HQ running so she'd been demoted to delivery girl today. After spending the last three hours running all over town dropping off and picking up, she was finally now on her way to her last stop: Brady's. She didn't even know what she was carting around. It had to be somewhat important or else Matthew wouldn't have been so adamant it all get done today, but it couldn't be too important or it wouldn't have been entrusted to someone so new to the campaign.

Aspyn double-checked the address as the taxi pulled to the curb. She expected something bigger, grander—something oozing wealth, not a charming town house on a trendy street in Rosslyn.

"Would you like me to wait again?" the cabbie asked.

She almost said yes, but she could easily get the Metro home from here. And, honestly, she'd spent enough time in this cab today. "Thanks, but no." She handed over the credit card Matthew had given her, tipped the driver well and hauled her packages up the front steps.

The day had turned out cool as fall finally took a strong hold on Virginia. Aspyn was thankful for the breeze that fanned her skin, because otherwise, her nerves would have her sweating. It was time to face Brady, and she still wasn't quite ready. She smoothed her shirt and sweater down over her hips, brushed some cab dirt off her jeans and adjusted the headband holding her hair back. She took a deep breath before ringing the bell. When she heard the doorknob click, she pasted a small, friendly, completely benign smile on her face. *I can do this.*

The look on Brady's face when he saw her would have been amusing if she hadn't held out small hope for something different.

Of course, *that* feeling was quickly swamped by her own surprise. She felt her jaw go slack and worried drool might be imminent.

Although she'd imagined what Brady would look like when he wasn't all buttoned up in a suit and tie, she wasn't prepared for *this*. Brady in a soft-from-many-washings T-shirt that strained over his shoulders and biceps. Faded jeans hugged his hips, the denim obviously well broken-in and frayed in places. And he was barefoot. Somehow, the sight of his toes nearly threw her over the edge. It seemed so…so…*natural.*

This was Brady, but not a Brady she'd seen before. This was the Brady she'd felt pressed against her and tasted on her lips. It was such a departure from the norm, but at the same time it made him seem so normal and magnified his inherent sex appeal.

And, *mercy,* he was very appealing.

Brady recovered first, the cool politico mask that fell into place a jarring contrast to the casual, easy appeal he otherwise presented. He stepped back to allow her entrance. "I didn't expect you to be playing courier this evening."

"Me, neither, but things were crazy without Lauren around, and I was considered the expendable one." Aspyn knew she was gawking, but she couldn't help it. She stepped inside and tried to act like she was admiring his foyer instead of him.

"It's been a crazy week all around. It's a bad time for anyone to get sick."

"Is that why you haven't been around HQ the last few days?"

A muscle in Brady's jaw twitched. "Yeah."

"Oh. That's good." She unloaded a few of the envelopes out of her bag and handed them over. Brady barely glanced at them before setting them aside on a marble-topped table. "Well, I'm glad *that* was important enough to send me running all over town on a Friday afternoon."

"Is there a problem I don't know about?"

Now was her chance. She took a deep breath and dug up some courage. "You tell me." Off his surprised look, she added, "The last time I saw you, you were kissing—"

He stepped back. "As I said, that shouldn't have happened."

"Why not?" She didn't want to sound petulant or needy, but damn it, she wanted answers.

He sighed and pushed the door closed. Then, facing her, he crossed his arms over his chest and leaned against the table. "Because you work for the campaign. So while that kiss shouldn't have happened—"

"So you've said."

"It had nothing to do with my schedule this week, *and* you can be assured it won't happen again."

The calm dismissal irked her. "Again I ask, why not? I'm really curious, because it's driving me crazy. Did I miss something? You seemed to be enjoying it at first." Brady coughed like he was choking. "And I *really* enjoyed it. Definitely an above average kiss as far—"

Brady finally caught his breath and cut her off. "Look, can we just forget it happened?"

"Sadly I can't. I've tried." She pushed her hands into her pockets. "And I can't go on like this. I need answers— *clear* answers about what that did or didn't mean. I have to know where to draw the lines."

Brady's face was unreadable, but his words were clipped and irritated. "It's inappropriate for me to get involved with anyone on the staff." If he got any more distant-sounding, he'd be phoning from the next county.

"So you're saying if I weren't on your staff—"

She didn't think it would be possible for Brady to sound more uninterested. She was quickly proven wrong. "No. I'm certainly not saying that."

"Oh." *It was me.* Her chest constricted in disappointment and shame. That kiss obviously didn't remotely affect Brady the way it had affected her. She was a fool to think otherwise. But it still hurt. "Okay then." She grasped for the tattered edges of her pride. "I guess we will just pretend it didn't happen then."

Like her life hadn't been through enough ups and downs already. She'd gone from mildly crushing on Brady to telling herself she couldn't have him at all, to that amazing kiss that had thrown her world sideways and now she'd just made a fool of herself. She definitely needed the weekend to get her head screwed back on straight or else she'd have to quit come Monday.

"I'm sorry—"

She held up a hand. The apology only made the situation worse. "No, I shouldn't have even brought it up. We're adults and—" She couldn't continue to face him, so she turned her back. "Whatever. It's all okay."

"Aspyn—"

She cut him off, unable to take any more. "I'm going to go now. Good night."

The doorknob turned easily and Aspyn kept her shoulders straight as she pulled. The door opened a few inches, then slammed shut. Confused, she lifted her eyes and saw Brady's hand pressed against the door.

A second later, she felt the heat on her back and knew Brady was only inches away. A shiver ran over her skin. *Stop. There's a reasonable explanation.* Careful not to move too far in his direction, Aspyn turned around and what she saw caused the shiver to turn sharp and needy.

This wasn't Dr.-Jekyll-Brady, but it wasn't Mr.-Hyde-Brady, either. *This* was the man who'd kissed her, and a small fire sparked to life low in her belly.

His eyes raked over her, but he didn't move otherwise. It made her nervous—in a good kind of way. "Brady?"

"That kiss was far above average, Aspyn." His words fanned the flames of that small fire, sending heat to her skin until she felt flushed. "And it shouldn't have happened." The words didn't hurt this time, probably because Brady was tracing a finger down the side of her face and she'd forgotten how to think. Or breathe.

And then neither one of those things mattered.

Brady's mouth was hot and hungry but unrushed, like he wanted to savor instead of devour. The sensation sapped her strength, causing her to wobble on her feet and grab Brady for support.

In return, she found herself pressed against the door for stability, the wood cool against her back and Brady hot against her front, and her hands were free to explore.

And, oh, what there was to discover. This time, she let her hands roam, carefully mapping the planes and ridges she'd only felt briefly before. Brady seemed to be doing the same, smoothing his hands over the small of her back, over her hips and her waist.

When Brady finally released her mouth and moved to the sensitive skin of her neck, she sucked in deep breaths and the rush of oxygen spurred her brain to shoot up one brief caution. *Be sure.*

"Brady…" Her voice felt thick and husky.

"Hmm?" he murmured before catching her earlobe in his teeth.

"You s-said…um…" She was having problems remembering English, and the featherlight kisses on her temples weren't helping. "That this wouldn't h-happen again."

Brady tensed briefly, then placed his forehead against hers. Eyes closed, he took a deep breath as a smile pulled at the corners of his mouth. "I was wrong."

"Oh." She couldn't manage much more.

He lifted his head and met her eyes. "Do you want me to stop?"

"God, no."

The smile grew bigger and he slid a hand under her shirt to the small of her back. His fingers traced the indention of her spine, causing goose bumps to rise on her skin. "Do you still want to leave?"

Well, that cut right to the chase. No dancing around. She liked that and it was an easy decision to make. "No."

MILLS
BOON

You can find all Mills & Boon titles at our webs
millsandboon.co.uk

For a limited time only, we are offering you an
EXCLUSIVE 15% OFF when you order online.
Simply enter the code **15NOV11** at the checkout.
But hurry, this offer ends on 30th November 2011.

PLUS, by ordering online you will receive all these extra benefits:

- Purchase new titles **1 MONTH AHEAD OF THE SHOPS**. Available in paperback and as eBooks!

- Order books from our huge backlist at a discounted price

- **Try before you buy** with Browse the Book

- Be the first to hear about exclusive offers in our eNewsletter

- Join the M&B community and discuss your favourite books with other readers

Terms and Conditions:
- Offer expires on 30th November 2011
- This offer cannot be used in conjunction with any other offer.
- Code can only be redeemed online at www.millsandboon.co.uk
- Exclusions apply
- Discount excludes delivery charge.

NOV1

His other hand joined the first, spreading heat across her back as he splayed his fingers over her skin. "Good."

She expected Brady to pick her up and move straight to the bedroom, but his lips found hers instead. Part of her protested, wanting more *now*, but Brady seemed in no hurry.

She tugged at his shirt until Brady finally lifted his arms and helped her pull it off. *Clothes were bad,* she decided as she ran her hands over his skin, because it was a crime against all womankind for Brady to keep that chest covered up. He sucked in his breath as her thumbs raked over his nipples.

"Your turn." He helped her shrug off the cardigan, which she'd quit needing the moment he touched her. Brady clasped her elbows and guided her hands over her head. He eased her shirt up slowly, the palms of his hands making it a long caress over her sides and arms as he pushed the fabric up and off. Her bra joined her shirt on the floor a second later, and she was bare to the waist.

She wasn't shy or modest or prudish—but Brady was so intense in his exploration, carefully tracing the swells of her breasts that she began to blush under the scrutiny. He mirrored her earlier move, brushing his thumbs over already tight nipples, causing her to gasp at the sensation.

She felt hot and light-headed and the tickle of Brady's fingers along the skin above the waistband of her jeans felt both far away and disturbingly immediate. It was too hard to focus when Brady kissed her, and Aspyn was more than happy to just lose herself in the madness of passion.

Brady hooked a hand under her butt and lifted her easily, settling her thighs on his hips and pulling her close. She finally had the contact she needed, hot and hard skin pressing against her breasts and stomach while crisp hairs tickled her nipples. She moved against him with a small groan, seeking more contact, and felt him smile against her neck.

When Brady finally moved, she sent up fervent thanks. She had no idea where they were headed, and she didn't care. Brief glimpses of a hallway, changes of light and finally cool softness against her back as Brady laid her on the bed.

She missed the wonderful weight of him between her thighs as he moved off her to shuck his clothes, but watching him strip *almost* made up for it. Her imagination hadn't come close to the reality of lean hips, powerful thighs and muscular calves. *My oh my.* She rolled onto her side, propped her head on her fist and took a long, lovely look.

Brady caught her staring and raised an eyebrow.

"Just admiring the view," she said.

"*My* view is a bit blocked at the moment. It hardly seems fair." He extended a hand to her.

"I'm all in favor of fairness and equality." She let Brady help her to her feet. She'd lost her shoes, but she had no memory of taking them off.

Brady flicked the snap of jeans and eased the zip open. He hooked two fingers in her belt loops and eased her jeans down, going to his knees as they reached the floor and she stepped out. She braced her hands on his shoulders as his mouth reversed the path of his hands until his lips reached the sensitive skin over her hip. His tongue traced along the top of her panties and she dug her fingers into the hard muscle, trying to steady herself but failing. She swayed when Brady's tongue slipped into her navel; by the time she regained her balance, her panties were around her ankles, and Brady was on his feet guiding her back on to the bed.

He stepped back and she could see the appreciation on his face. It made her feel sexy, powerful. "This is a much better view now. Beautiful landscape."

"You're making me blush."

"That's new."

"It certainly doesn't happen often."

Brady's grin was the sexiest thing she'd ever seen, and every nerve in her body screamed for attention. Deep breaths were impossible as Brady joined her on the bed, hovering over her on all fours. His head dipped to her breast, teasing her nipple until her back arched in pleasure. "I take that as a challenge," he said, before moving his mouth to her other breast. "And I love a challenge."

Brady was a driven, determined, goal-oriented man. Aspyn knew that from working with him. She respected that. But when Brady's hand slipped between her thighs and his fingers pressed inside, she was thankful for it, too.

As the first little tremors started to shake her body, she amended that thought.

Very, *very*, thankful.

CHAPTER SIX

BRADY had never been much of a rule-breaker. With two younger brothers raising hell and living in hot water, *someone* had to be the responsible one. But breaking a rule he'd laid down himself? That was a first. Sleeping with an employee was just asking for all kinds of trouble and scandal and lawsuits, but, right now, Brady couldn't give a damn.

Aspyn sighed, sending a warm draft across his chest, then rolled off him. Once on her back, she stretched— probably completely unaware of the erotic picture it created—then flipped to her stomach and propped herself on her elbows.

She flashed him a cheeky smile. "Well, my ego feels better now."

That was a change from "Was it good for you?" "Just your ego?"

"Okay, my everything feels much better now, but my ego really needed the reassurance."

"Because…?"

"Because it's taken quite a beating from you recently." She trailed a hand over his chest. "A hot guy—who's not married or gay—totally immune to all my feminine wiles. Cue the battered ego."

"Then I apologize." He tugged at one of her curls and

smiled as it sprung back into place. "I did not mean to cast your wiles into doubt. They are all in proper working order."

"Why, thank you, Mr. Marshall." She exaggerated her drawl and batted her eyelashes. "You certainly know how to put a smile on a girl's face."

"My pleasure."

"Oh, I hope so. I'd hate to think that was a chore for you. And talk about ego-destroying…"

The laugh felt good. Strange, but good. Aspyn put everything in a different light with her approach to life. Even sex, it seemed.

Aspyn made a face and smacked him playfully. "Maybe I should have heeded Lauren's warnings."

Lauren and warnings were two things he really didn't want to discuss in his bed. But as always, Aspyn drew the question out anyway. "Lauren warned you? About what?"

"Oh, it was a very nice lecture, delivered with only the best intentions I'm sure, basically telling me not to get any ideas about you because you don't 'fish in the company pond.'"

"Lauren is right." Aspyn raised an eyebrow at him. "Usually," he amended. "But it seems there's an exception to every rule. I get the feeling you're the exception to a lot of rules."

She grinned. "Only sometimes. But I totally respect that position, you know. Office romances are tricky at best and disruptive when they go bad. A general moratorium is good, sound management policy."

He agreed completely… "Yet here we are."

"Indeed." The hand on his chest eased down and her fingers circled his navel. "Lauren said she'd seen it before and just wanted to save me some heartbreak down the road."

Uh-oh. "Well…"

Aspyn burst into laughter. "Oh, my. Look at your face." She pushed up to a seated position and dragged the sheet across her lap, either unaware or uncaring that the view of her breasts was still distracting. "Let's not panic here, okay? I like you. You're smart and you're hot and what you just did was nothing short of amazing, but, it's just sex. *Great* sex," she amended, "but it's still just sex." She laughed. "Have I shocked you?"

That was a refreshing view. A tiny bit insulting, and not one he'd never heard from a woman currently in his bed. There was nothing in her voice or body language to make him think her casual attitude was masking something else or fishing for more. "Once again, you have managed to surprise me."

"Poor Brady." She ran a hand over his jaw. "It must be so hard to be a handsome, charming, well-connected eligible bachelor in this town."

Was she mocking him? "Well, when you say it like *that*…"

"No, I'm serious. I've seen how people treat you, heard how they talk about you. I can connect the dots. I bet women are lined up with nets and cages and stun guns trying to tie you down. Lauren's warning was probably more about protecting you than any concern about me." She laughed and lay down next to him. "I can actually picture you being pursued by this pack of women in wedding dresses trying force you to the altar. And this—" her hand moved to his hip "—could be construed as a major step in that direction. *If* that's what the woman was after."

Aspyn was uncomfortably astute. "So you see the problem."

"Yeah. I promise you, though, I'm not after anything other than your body."

It was an erotic statement—and it slammed into him—but… "Should I be offended by that?"

"No. That—what we just did—was awesome. In fact, I'd like to do it again. Soon, and often, if possible. So I'll tell you something to relieve your mind and clear your overdeveloped conscience."

His body picked up on the "again" and "soon" part of her statement. The languid feeling in his blood had now been completely replaced by interest and heat. He had to force himself to focus. "And that would be…?"

She looked him straight in the eye and wrinkled her nose. "I don't want to marry you."

Until this moment, Brady hadn't realized it was possible to be relieved *and* insulted at the same time. The conflicting feelings made no sense, but he was starting to get used to that confused feeling where Aspyn was concerned. With her, *nothing* was what he expected. He kept his voice light and tried to sound amused. "I don't believe I asked you to."

"Good. Then we're clear." She snuggled down next to him and rested her head on his chest like she hadn't just thrown a verbal grenade. Aspyn fit into him like a puzzle piece, letting her leg drape over his so she could run her toes over his calf like a sexy promise.

He should let it go, but he couldn't. "Out of simple curiosity—which I really must learn to rein in around you—is it the institution or me, personally, you object to?"

She put a fist on his chest and balanced her chin on it as she grinned at him again. "Oh, I'm sure you'll make some nice girl from the right family a fine husband one day, but I don't believe in marriage."

She said it matter-of-factly, like she didn't expect to have to clarify or justify. Though he knew he shouldn't and he'd probably regret it later, he couldn't help asking, "In theory or in practice?"

"Both. It's a false construct that abuses the entire idea of love. If two people want to be together, then they should be. But not because some piece of paper says so. That's taking the easy way out. Commitment is demonstrated by waking up every morning and *choosing* to be with that person because it's what makes you happy, not just because you're 'married.' A forced commitment is worthless. Love is staying when you could just as easily leave."

Just when he thought Aspyn couldn't get more surprising. "Didn't you claim to be an optimist?"

"I am. Loving someone is optimism at its best. But love shouldn't come with strings attached, and they call marriage 'tying the knot' for a reason. My parents have been together for over thirty years because every day they decide they *want* to be together."

"Your parents aren't married?" When would he stop being surprised at everything that came out of her mouth?

"No. They took the name Breedlove shortly before I was born because they were becoming a family and that's what families do—breed love. They're happy and one of the strongest couples I've ever seen, but they don't need paper to prove it." She slithered on top of him, giving him skin-to-skin contact from her breasts to her toes before tucking her knees around his hips and pushing up to straddle him. "But we are talking about sex. Sex between two healthy, mature adults. And that has nothing to do with love or commitment or—horrors!—marriage." Aspyn splayed her hands on his stomach and let her thumbs trace around the edges of his navel. "Since I can assure you I'm not looking for strings or rings, can I keep my job and still have sex with you?"

Aspyn's bluntness could hit hard sometimes. When combined with the carnal look and the feeling of being pressed against her slippery warmth, it was all he could do to not shift her the necessary inch or two and slide home. He reached for a condom, moved her just enough to cover himself, then placed her back in her earlier position. Then he addressed the other half of her statement while running his thumbs along the insides of her thighs. Two could play this game. "You're concerned about your job?"

"Yeah." A small shiver ran over her and she rocked against him. "It's been difficult the last few days because I didn't know where things stood with us after that kiss, and it would have been easier to just quit than continue on like that. But then I realized I didn't *want* to quit. I like working for the campaign." She slid her hands up to his chest as she spoke. "And trust me, *that* surprises me a hell of a lot more than it could surprise you."

He mirrored her movement, cupping her breasts in his hands and massaging gently. "Your job is only temporary."

"Mmm-hmm." The sound was one of both agreement and pleasure. "But I'm learning a lot, and maybe I'll want to find another job in the political world when this is done."

He could salve his conscience with that. Only a few people knew the truth behind her position and none of them would be spreading that information around. Meanwhile, Aspyn was smart and learning quickly. The experience she was getting would be valuable to her. "But if I want to keep *my* job in politics, I can't let it be known that I sleep with members of my staff."

"Of course not. And I wouldn't want possible future employers to think I'm using something other than my brain to get ahead. Reputation is everything in politics, you know." Aspyn moaned softly and rocked her hips against him.

"You *are* learning fast."

"It'll be a real challenge, but I can probably keep it under control in front of other people." Aspyn lifted her hips, repositioned herself and slid slowly down until her skin met his again, encasing him in slick heat that sent a shudder through him. Her eyes closed as that shudder then moved through her, and she bit her lip as she savored it. Opening her eyes, she met his gaze squarely. "Can you?"

He held her hips as she started to move and her breath began to come in short, breathy gasps, punctuated by tiny cries of pleasure. "I told you I love a challenge."

"Glad…to…hear…it," she said between moans. Then her back arched as tremors took over and her muscles contracted. Reality dimmed around the edges as Aspyn came apart with a shout, and he exploded with a force that had him seeing stars.

Aspyn wanted to bang her head against something hard. It would be infinitely more productive than continuing the email exchange with this man in Fredericksburg. She despised the fact she was now the one providing vague, useless responses to someone who obviously cared deeply about protecting the coastal regions, but honestly, there was no good way to tell someone that their proposed solutions were unfeasible, unsustainable and quite frankly, insane.

"You okay?" Matthew propped a hip on her desk next to her keyboard.

"Just frustrated. This guy is just…" She shook her head.

"I told you not to engage."

"I know, but people deserve explanations—otherwise they get frustrated and angry and think I'm not listening. They mean well and they care, but they just don't get it. They want easy answers and quick fixes, but those don't exist. Their 'solutions' would only create a new problem somewhere else."

"How ironic this situation must be for you. Welcome to the other side of the fence, Aspyn."

She shot him a dirty look that only caused him to laugh before she turned back to her monitor and tried to decide what to say to this man next.

"How about we go get a drink?"

She sighed. "Thanks, but I'm fine at the moment. I'll watch the phones while you're gone, though."

"If I go alone, that rather defeats the purpose."

"What?" She could tell by the look on his face she'd missed something. "I'm sorry, but that irony, as you called it, is making me grouchy and distracted."

Matthew's smile was slightly shy. "Then let me clarify. Would you like to have a drink *with me* tonight?"

She couldn't. Brady was on his way back from an overnight trip to Norfolk. She needed to catch up on a few more emails, proofread her report, get home to shower and change and pick up Thai food on her way to Brady's. She didn't have time to have a drink with Matthew. "Sorry, but I can't."

Matthew's smile faded and the disappointment on his face clued her in a moment too late. *Damn.* "Can't or won't?"

Double damn. Was there a nice way to do this? She didn't really have much practice letting guys down easy.

Honesty was always her first choice, but Matthew was a nice guy and she wanted to keep a good working relationship with him. She edged around the truth. "A little of both."

"I see."

"Please don't be hurt or angry. You're nice and you're cute and you're funny, but I just don't feel *that* way toward you. And we work together. It could make things…awkward around here." *You seem to be doing okay with Brady* a little voice whispered.

"The election isn't far off. We won't be 'around here' much longer."

"True." Just three more weeks. Brady's schedule would only get more crazy until then, and they were already having a tough time carving out any time alone. But it was worth it. The past week had been insane yet fantastic. She was running on little sleep most days, and their need for discretion made for some interesting finagling, but it was still worth it.

"Maybe if you took me up on that drink, you could find out if you…"

"Matthew, I'm flattered, but no." *Firm, yet friendly.*

Matthew's mouth twisted and his voice turned caustic. "He'll never notice you, you know."

"Excuse me?"

"It's obvious that you have the hots for Brady, but if you're holding out hope he's going to suddenly notice you as something other than a cog in this machine, you're wasting your time."

Aspyn bit her tongue. It was a good thing she didn't hope for a future career in espionage. She sucked at any attempt to be covert or stealthy. But if Matthew thought her "hots" were one-sided, that was good. A little embarrassing, but still good. At least no one knew she and Brady were sleeping together. "I appreciate your concern, but…"

"I get it. I understand why women fall for him. But take some advice from someone who's been around this game longer than you have?" He stood and leaned over her. "Politics can make strange bedfellows in the literal sense, too, because it's all about making the most of moments and opportunities. In order to do that, people have to be expendable. You might be an optimist now, but politics eats optimists for breakfast. I like the Marshalls—Brady, too— but they didn't get where they are today without using up and discarding more than a few people."

She couldn't stop her shoulders from stiffening. "Wow, that's a harsh thing to say about the people who pay your salary."

Matthew shrugged. "That's not a condemnation. That's just the way this works. There's no such thing as harmless crushes or easy affairs in D.C. Someone *will* use it against you."

There was no good response to that statement. "I'll try to keep that in mind for the future."

"Yeah. I recommend you do. Especially if you think you want any kind of future around Capitol Hill." Matthew's parting shot didn't mask his hurt and anger, and he stayed on the far side of the room after that.

First Lauren and now Matthew? Ugh. She'd believe Lauren was working with Brady's best interests in mind, and Matthew might be coming from a place of jealousy and disappointment, but both of them seemed to believe *she* was the only one in any danger. It was both funny and embarrassing. And slightly insulting when she really thought about it. She and Brady were from different worlds, true, but being told she was expendable and not good enough had her hackles up.

Why do I care what they think? She and Brady were having a good time. No one was being used—or maybe they were using each other. Politics might make strange bedfellows, but this wasn't politics. It simply was what it was. Nothing more, nothing less.

As long as they both knew that, there wasn't a problem.

"Tell me again how you're not sleeping with Aspyn." Ethan's voice was just loud enough to be heard over the music, but not loud enough to carry to others' ears. "And just for laughs, try to make me believe it."

Brady kept his eyes on the crowd. With Congress adjourned until after the election, this was very much a collection of the local movers-and-shakers and the atmosphere was deceptively festive. However… "This is not the time or the place to have that kind of conversation."

"You're the one who brought her. You're practically advertising it."

There must be at least three hundred people in the room. Two hundred and fifty of them probably hadn't noticed Aspyn was even present, and those that had were too busy furthering their own interests to care about one activist-turned-campaign staffer. And it wasn't like they arrived together. "Aspyn hasn't had a chance to meet Dad yet—"

"Lucky her," Ethan mumbled into his glass.

"So," Brady continued like Ethan hadn't said anything, "this is a simple, low-pressure way to accomplish that. And since Aspyn has been toying with the idea of getting more involved with politics, this is a good way for her to network." He watched as Aspyn laughed over something with a Supreme Court clerk. "Plus she's enjoying herself. Someone here should."

"At least you're not denying it. Avoidance I can respect, but denial would be beneath you."

Brady turned on him. "Why are you here anyway? I thought you weren't coming."

Ethan shrugged. "Ah, the Grands can be very persuasive—especially when they double-team. Like I'm going to disappoint Nana? Lily would kill me."

He looked pointedly at the empty space around them. "Yet Lily's not here."

"She's not a Marshall yet, so she intends to use that excuse for as long as she can. Nice try changing the subject, but we're still on the topic of Aspyn."

"Aspyn is none of your business."

Shaking his head and *tsking* quietly, Ethan pretended to think. "Interesting. See, I got this lecture back when Lily and I first got together about all the problems and pitfalls awaiting those who date outside their tax bracket. There was something about scandals and lawsuits... Hmm, now who delivered that lecture?" Ethan paused, then pinned him with a stare. "Oh, yeah. You."

He didn't need reminding. "Well, you obviously didn't listen."

That earned him a chuckle. "And that surprises you? Anyway, you were wrong."

"I was not wrong. In fact, I stand behind everything I said. It can be a problem."

"Your relationship with Aspyn seems rather hypocritical then."

"Aspyn and I have an understanding. This is a different situation." He could split hairs with the best of them, it seemed.

The look on Ethan's face said he was completely aware of what Brady was doing. "Really, now. How very interesting."

"Not really. Your relationship with Lily could have blown up in your face—and it nearly did. You just got lucky."

Ethan grinned. "Very lucky. And speaking of getting lucky..." He scanned the room until he found Aspyn.

"Look, there's Granddad with Senator Caffery. Caffery's still bitter he spent twenty years in the Senate and remained the 'Junior Senator.' Maybe we should go save Granddad."

"You go save him." Ethan flagged down a passing server and handed over his empty glass. "I'm going to go introduce myself to Aspyn."

Good God, there was no telling what Ethan would say to her. Brady sighed. He had no choice but to follow in his brother's wake.

Aspyn's smile widened as she saw him approaching, but it remained cool and polite. She had learned fast, and every day Aspyn seemed to fit in better, but without losing her identity in the process. She'd taken the standard D.C. cocktail party uniform and made it her own, choosing a forties retro-inspired dress and taming her curls into soft waves around her face. It was appropriate, yet totally Aspyn at the same time. She looked stunning—but he'd told her that already—and he was amazed and proud at how well she was handling the crush of people and power and money.

"Aspyn, this is my brother Ethan."

She shot him a look at his surly tone, but hers was the perfect mix of polite and friendly. "I certainly see the family resemblance. I've heard so much about you, Ethan, that it's nice to finally meet you."

"I could say the same about you." Ethan leaned closer to Aspyn. "Don't trust anything Brady tells you about me."

Her head cocked to the side in a perfect imitation of confusion. "That's funny, Brady said the same thing about you."

Brady bit back a laugh, but Ethan took it in stride. "Quick and loyal *and* pretty. I approve, Brady."

Aspyn blinked. "Excuse me?" She looked at Brady for help.

He shook his head. "Just ignore him. I do."

Ethan, however, wouldn't be ignored. He snagged two glasses of champagne from a waiter and handed one to Aspyn. "Are you having a good time, Aspyn?"

"I am. It's not at all what I expected." She leaned forward and wrinkled her nose. "Name tags would be *very* helpful, though."

"What happened?"

"I didn't recognize Representative Delany and kind of told him that the groundwater protections in the new House bill were a complete joke."

Brady burst out laughing, causing Aspyn to frown at him. At Ethan's questioning look, she confessed her sin in hushed tones. "Mr. Delany wrote that bill."

Ethan toasted her. "Good for you, Aspyn. D.C. needs more people unafraid to speak the truth."

Aspyn looked a little embarrassed. "Well, it's certainly easier when you don't know who you're talking to."

"Trust my grandsons to find the prettiest woman in the room and monopolize her time." Granddad reached for Aspyn's hand and clasped it in both of his. Smiling at her the whole time, Granddad barely turned his head in Brady's direction as he ordered, "Brady, humor an old man and introduce me to this delightful young lady."

Ethan rolled his eyes and Brady didn't bother to hide his grin. Granddad's charm was legendary—if bordering on corny—and Aspyn didn't seem immune. "Granddad, this is Aspyn Breedlove, who recently joined the campaign staff. Aspyn, this is my grandfather, Porter Marshall, who was a very good senator before he became a terrible flirt."

Aspyn frowned in his direction before turning her smile on Granddad. "It's an honor to meet you, Senator. Your work on human rights and environmental policy is legendary and an example all public servants should strive to emulate."

Ethan shot Brady an impressed look. Aspyn was *good*.

Granddad beamed. "I like this one. Smart as well as beautiful. You need to hold on to her, Brady."

That coughing to his left came from Ethan. Both Aspyn and Granddad turned toward him, and Ethan recovered with a "Something stuck in my throat. Sorry." Brady tried to stare him into good behavior, but the idiot merely shrugged.

"I'm afraid Brady's going to have a hard time getting rid of me," Aspyn said in a conspiratorial whisper. "I know I haven't been around that long, but the whole experience has been amazing and so much more fun than I imagined. I'm learning so much, and I'm very excited to see what's next."

Ethan made another choking noise, and only their audience kept Brady from going for his brother's throat. Ethan must have realized how close to death he was this time and turned his attention to the other side of the room. "Look. There's Russ Andrews. I need to speak to him. Aspyn, it was really nice meeting you," he finished, barely keeping his amusement out of his voice.

Aspyn looked slightly confused and Brady knew he'd have some explaining to do later. Granddad, however, defused the moment by patting Aspyn's hand and shaking his head. "Ethan's an odd one sometimes. He gets that from his grandmother."

Then, with timing too perfect to be coincidental, his father joined their little group. "I'll be sure to tell Mother you said that." His father put on his best senator smile. "Now, who is this young lady?"

"Dad, this is Aspyn Breedlove. Aspyn, my father, Senator Douglas Marshall." He watched carefully as they shook hands and Aspyn mentioned again how much she enjoyed working for the campaign, but there was no glimmer of recognition in his father's eyes. *Damn.* Once the impetus to get Aspyn off the news and under their wing had passed, Dad had completely and conveniently forgotten she existed.

And Aspyn was quickly figuring that out. Her smile lost its brightness and shadows clouded her eyes.

"Dad, we were definitely right to bring Aspyn on board. The outpouring of comments from across the state—and across the country, really—has been unprecedented. People seem to like knowing they have a real person listening to their concerns." Still nothing but generic nods from his father, and even Granddad was beginning to frown in his direction. *So much for subtle hints.* Brady forced himself to laugh. "Aspyn should be careful or else half of Congress will be handcuffing themselves to her to prove they're listening, too."

Finally his father caught on. "It was a rather unorthodox situation that brought you to us, Miss Breedlove, but it's wonderful having you on staff. You've definitely blown the dust off and shaken up the way we thought to do things."

"Thank you. It's been an eye-opening experience." Although she kept her voice steady, he could see the disappointment and disillusionment dawning in her eyes. He wanted to kick his father for hurting Aspyn like that. And he wanted to kick himself because deep down he'd known this was a possibility and he'd still let Aspyn get in this position.

"Glad to hear it. And thank you for your hard work." Thankfully his father was ready to move on to the next circle of people, and he made his goodbyes.

Granddad smiled supportively in Aspyn's direction. "I think I need to go speak to Justice Williams. Wonderful to meet you, my dear." He gave Brady a look that clearly said "Smooth it over" as he left.

From the look on her face, smoothing it over would be difficult. "Dad's impressed and Granddad really likes you. I think you can consider yourself a success tonight."

"Your grandfather is wonderful, and Ethan seems nice." She leveled a stern look at him. "The senator isn't impressed, though. He doesn't know me from Adam's housecat. You could have just *told* me, you know, and I wouldn't have pushed so hard to get to meet him."

"Dad's just busy. He's got a lot of people working for him, so don't take it personally that he couldn't place you. He forgets my name sometimes, too," he teased, but the joke fell flat.

"I see," she said in the tone he'd learned meant she was actually still drawing her conclusions and not liking them.

"Remember how I told you campaigns and governing were two different things? Dad's been focused on the governing part recently. Now that Congress is on break, he'll be shifting focus to the campaigning. If you'd met him a few days from now, when he's firmly in campaign mode, I'm sure he would have placed you instantly."

"If you say so," she said, relenting only the smallest bit. "I'd hate to think I sold my soul to the devil and he didn't even appreciate it."

"What?"

"Nothing." She shook her head and drank deeply from her glass. "It's just hard to adjust my thinking sometimes."

"My father is not the nicest man in the world, and not one you'd want to hang out with socially, but he's not actually evil. Things aren't always either/or."

"I know that. It's just culture shock. This side of the fence isn't exactly what I thought it would be sometimes."

"I know. But you're doing brilliantly." He wanted to reach for her, but there were far too many people around for him to cross that boundary. "And besides, after the impression you've made tonight, you're going to have bigger, better connections than just the current Senator Marshall."

She lifted an eyebrow. "I thought the Marshalls were the biggest, best connection a girl could have in Washington."

"We like to say that, but, in reality, it's probably not true."

"Liar." But she laughed, and her mood was shifting.

"I'm proud of you. You're working the crowd like a pro. And you look amazing."

"Thanks." She lifted a hand to adjust his lapel, but dropped it as she looked around and realized she shouldn't. "You're looking very 'future senatorial material' tonight."

"Then I must go change immediately." He was only half-kidding.

She dropped her voice a notch. "I don't know about that. That look seems to work for you. You've got a vibe going that's very sexy." She giggled. "I never thought I'd ever find anything about Congress 'sexy.'"

This was not an appropriate venue for Aspyn to be talking about "sexy." His body was already on alert, and he had at least another hour of schmoozing before he could leave. It was a dangerous conversation to be having, but, as always, Aspyn seemed to cause him to break all kinds of rules. So he grinned and said, "Wealth and power are strong aphrodisiacs."

"You think?"

"Of course. How do you think all these balding, paunchy old men get such hot young mistresses?"

Aspyn nodded slowly, a smile curling her top lip. She waved him closer, and he bent his head forward—and the clear view down her cleavage didn't help his current situation any—so she could speak quietly next to his ear. "And here I was just wanting you for your hot body and the great sex."

All of his blood rushed south at her husky tone. Aspyn stepped back before he could grab her and drag her behind the ficus and palms arranged in the corner. With a toss of her curls, she walked away, obviously pleased at having the last word.

It was several more minutes before he could rejoin the party.

CHAPTER SEVEN

ASPYN cursed as she eyeballed the burned crust of her quiche. So much for her attempts at domesticity. She had her strengths, but cooking wasn't one of them. Normally she'd accept that with no problem, but today had sucked all the way around, and this was just the topper. She refilled her wineglass and considered just going back to her place and crawling under the covers until tomorrow.

It was a tempting thought, but she wasn't a quitter. She glanced at the laptop on the table and the email she needed to answer. She wasn't a quitter, but there was no shame in being a procrastinator. She needed more time to figure out how she was going to explain all of this since she still couldn't quite explain it to herself satisfactorily.

She went looking for another bottle of wine as she heard Brady's keys in the door.

"Hi." He looked tired, rumpled from travel and magically delicious. "Something smells good." He gave her a quick kiss and loosened his tie. He peeked over her shoulder at the stove and a crease formed on his forehead. "Oh, that's a…"

"Real men can eat quiche. And I promise not to tell anyone that you did." She struggled with the corkscrew until Brady took it out of her hand and easily uncorked the wine. For Gaia's sake, she was such a disaster she couldn't even open a wine bottle. "How were the good people of Lynchburg and Appomattox today?"

"Happier to see us than expected. Taylor was hoping to take that area, but polls had it leaning toward us." Brady pulled a beer from the fridge and leaned against the counter. "After today, I'm thinking it's definitely in our column."

"Our favorables are up across the board," she said, refilling her glass. "Taylor lacks any substantial support from women or Independents, and he's losing ground with his base. His internal polls show him shedding moderate voters like a long-haired cat in a heat wave."

That brought a smile to Brady's face, but not for the reason she thought at first. He hooked a finger into her belt loop and pulled her toward him until their legs touched. "You are amazingly sexy when you toss around words like 'favorables' and 'internal polls.'"

Heat curled through her belly. She finished the job of loosening his tie and slid it out of his collar. She tried for a seductive purr. "Then just wait until you hear my analysis of demographic breakdowns across economic lines."

He gripped her hips and pulled her into full contact with the hard lines of his body. "That's so hot," he growled and kissed her until her knees went weak.

Her mood was improving rapidly.

Brady grinned when he released her. He tucked one hand in the back pocket of her jeans to hold her against him and reached for his beer with the other. "How was your day?"

"Eh." She shrugged and toyed with his shirt buttons.

"What's that supposed to mean?"

"Nothing." She sighed. "I'm just grumbling. You hungry?"

"Not hungry enough to change the subject." He forced her chin up so she met his eyes. "What's wrong?"

Did she even want to get into it? Brady's expectant stare implied she didn't have much of a choice. "My parents finally got back to Port-au-Prince and Internet access. They emailed me today."

"I would think that was a good thing."

"It is. The water reclamation system they've been working on is finally functional and they've been reassigned to one of the free clinics in the city. They're going to go on a supply delivery over the next few days, but sometime next week they'll be back in the land of Internet access. They'll be in contact a lot more." She forced herself to smile as she said it.

"And yet you still haven't told me how that's connected to your grumbling."

"Well, they were a little surprised to hear about my new job."

He chuckled. "I can understand that."

"No. You can't," she snapped. Brady looked at her, expecting more explanation and she regretted losing even that small grip on her temper. She took a deep breath. "My parents have a deep distrust of the U.S. government. They think corporate interests have corrupted the entire system and Congress is… Well, it's…" *There was no nice way to say this.*

Brady picked up on her hesitation. "Spit it out. I doubt there's anything you could say that I haven't heard. I'm not easily offended."

"Fine. In a nutshell, Congress is evil, politicians are beyond redemption and the whole damn system went off the rails a long time ago." Her parents' voices rang in her ears as she spoke. "The will and interest of the people is being ignored at best and intentionally thwarted at worst. They're focused on humanitarian efforts now, but my parents have forty-plus years of railing against the government and its policies under their belts. And now…" She blew out her breath in defeat.

Brady nodded. "Their daughter has crossed to the Dark Side."

"Not in so many words, but, yeah, that's the general gist."

"Back up and tell me exactly what they said." He unbuttoned his cuffs and rolled up his sleeves like he intended to physically work the problem. It was rather sweet.

Aspyn swirled the wine in her glass. Something about the movement calmed her thoughts a little. "Their communication access is sketchy. I last talked to them right about the time the whole Listen To Us circus was in full swing, and they were so proud. There I was, the face of something they'd been angry about for years."

"And you didn't tell them when you joined the campaign."

She shook her head. "I didn't see the sense in doing it immediately. I thought I'd wait and see how it worked out. But my parents are well-known in certain circles, and people in those circles rushed to contact my parents with the news of their progeny's betrayal. Electronic communication might be iffy, but the grapevine seems to be in full working order."

"Do they *see* it as a betrayal?"

"Well, right now they're slightly confused. They want confirmation and explanations of what they're hearing."

"So they're not actually calling you some kind of traitor to the cause."

"No, there's no condemnation. Yet, at least. They're my parents and they love me regardless, but it's not that simple." That sick feeling Brady's presence had helped hold at bay rolled through her stomach again. "They have every right to be horrified. I'm helping to promote an institution they see as systemically corrupt and morally wrong. I'm supposed to be fighting for change, not helping dig the trenches even deeper."

Brady's eyebrows went up in shock. "Is that how you see what you're doing?"

"I still believe our government is…not always acting with the best interest of the people foremost in mind," she hedged. This was Brady's family—and him, by association—she was disparaging. He may have heard it all before, but she didn't want to pile on. "But I also now understand a little better how it all works and how important it is to work within the system for change instead of just demanding that it change."

"That sounds perfectly rational. And smart." Brady moved to stand in front of her and rubbed his hands over her arms in support. "You haven't turned your back on your beliefs, Aspyn. You're still working toward your goal—the same goal they instilled in you—only via a different route than assumed."

She'd told herself that, and it had even sounded good, too, until Mom's email showed up, full of questions and worries of what she'd gotten involved in. "You know how I told you my parents were 'true believers'? That's an understatement. They're so far out there, they make the fringe look moderate."

"But you are not your parents. You're allowed to have

your own beliefs and make your own decisions. You don't have to follow the path they chose."

She was freaking out and needed someone to come along. Brady's calm, rational approach caused her to snap. "Oh, you're one to talk. You toe the party line and recite the talking points—same as your father and grandfather. And they expect you to assume the throne one day. Can you honestly say that your family would be fine with you suddenly switching political parties? Or if you decided to forego the family 'business' altogether and become an organic dairy farmer in Wisconsin? That's what I'm talking about here."

Brady dropped his hands and his jaw tightened. Aspyn regretted the barb, and, thankfully, Brady didn't take the bait. "My family would be disappointed, of course. But as long as I did it for reasons that were important to me, they'd understand. They wouldn't disown me."

"Yes, but they would still *feel* betrayed. Or that they'd failed somehow. That's the whole purpose of instilling your values in your children. You think they're important values and it's what you live your life by. Having your child reject that or betray it?" The throbbing behind her left eye grew stronger. "You might still love your child, but you're going to have a hard time feeling proud of them."

Brady nodded slowly. "And that's what you want. Your parents to be proud of you."

"Of course. Don't you?"

"They will be proud of you. You're working hard and…"

"Turning my back on everything I was taught to believe."

"Focus, Aspyn. You still have a mission. A good one. It's not like you're burning down a rain forest or hunting baby seals."

"I really hate it when you patronize me, Brady Marshall." She pushed off the counter and started to pace. "There's more to object to than the act itself. It's the beliefs that *allow* those things to happen that are the root of the problem. I'll never be as dedicated as my parents. I'm too selfish and spoiled by hot running water and broadband Internet access to go to the extremes they did. I've accepted that and so have they. But working for your father's campaign is supporting a status quo that they will see as just as harmful as allowing clear-cutting of a rain forest."

"No offense, but your parents sound like they lack perspective."

She stopped midpace. "Oh, *please*. No one sees the bigger picture like Lydia and Allen Breedlove. They could connect the shoes on your feet to destruction of wild tiger habitats without pausing for a breath. Never play Six Degrees of Eco-Socio-Political Separation with them. You will lose."

"Noted." Brady hooked her belt again and pulled her back close. "Who or what are you actually mad at? Them? Me? Yourself? Tigers?"

The touch of humor helped Aspyn reel herself back in. "You know, I just don't know anymore. I've been trying to sort that out for hours now and all I've gotten is a headache." She scrubbed a hand over her face and rubbed her temples. "I thought I'd justified everything to myself and was good with where I stood. But now I just don't know. Maybe I am a sellout."

"You are not a sellout." He put a finger under her chin, lifting it, and forced her to meet his eyes. "Your passion and beliefs are still as strong as ever. And I really think once you explain to your parents what you're actually doing, they'll see it that way as well." Warmth moved through her, and the sick feeling abated in its wake. Then Brady cleared his throat and raised an eyebrow at her. "And that's not the party line, by the way."

She winced. "I'm sorry about that jab. Upholding the family legacy is an honorable thing—especially when you love it as much as you do. I'm just feeling a bit sensitive about it at the moment." She laughed. "I'm sure you couldn't tell *that*."

Brady handed her her wineglass and she took a grateful swallow, letting the smooth taste soothe her jagged nerves. "Once when I was frustrated, Granddad reminded me that even slow progress was forward progress. You've encouraged people to speak out directly to the ones who actually can make changes instead of just railing at the skies. The knowledge you've picked up can be shared with other organizations to help them work the system for change. That's not selling out. That's reality."

She laughed. "Actually that's optimism."

"Perish the thought." Brady smiled. "Maybe you're rubbing off on me."

"Well, your secret is safe with me."

"Good, because we can't let word get out that I'm an optimistic, quiche-eating kind of guy who is now rather oddly worried about his wardrobe destroying tiger habitats. I'd lose all my street cred."

She snorted. "Are you trying to imply the Capitol Building is its own 'hood?"

"Two powerful and rival groups fighting for dominance and control, cutthroat deals, the struggle to get on top and wield the power... The analogy doesn't take a great leap of logic."

"No, just a huge ego and an overinflated sense—"

He kissed her to stop her words. "Admit it, you're starting to love it for exactly what it is. A challenge."

"No, that's why *you* love it. I tolerate it because I have no choice but to accept how things work."

"Ah, Aspyn, you're missing the best part then. It's such a pity." Brady's body belied even the mock sympathy in his voice. His hands were back in her pockets, squeezing and caressing, and she could feel the direction his thoughts were headed as he grew hard against her. Her thigh muscles loosened in response. "Are you hungry?" he asked.

"Not at the moment." She raised up on tiptoes and pressed herself fully against him.

Brady made a humming sound low in his throat.

Leaning close to his ear, she whispered, "Swing voters. Margin of error. Rallying the base."

With a laugh, Brady swept her off her feet and carried her to the bedroom.

Later that night, snuggled under Brady's duvet with his leg thrown over her, Aspyn couldn't quiet the thoughts his offhand comment stirred up in her mind.

Reputation—street cred—meant a hell of a lot. She knew that even before she got mixed up with the Marshalls. But Brady had nothing to fear; he radiated power like a thousand-watt lightbulb. Blinding. Unable to be ignored or dismissed. No one would ever mistake him for anything other than exactly what he was. And he knew it.

She used to feel that way: secure in herself, honest in how she led her life, and perfectly willing to let the rest of the world deal with that however best they could.

But something had shifted inside her now, and her skin didn't fit quite right anymore. *Had* she been lured to the Dark Side? She had twinges of conscience that she might only be justifying her actions because the pleasures—all of them, but Brady mainly, she admitted—were too seductive and enjoyable to give up. Sleeping with the enemy seemed far too apt a description, especially since he was proving addictive on his own.

Had her perspective shifted? Was she really seeing a bigger picture now, or was she only focusing on what she wanted to? Had she set herself up to be used and discarded by the system, destroying *her* reputation to the point no one would ever take her seriously again? And if so, would she have any chance of redemption in the eyes of those who saw her as a traitor?

The ramifications were becoming clear just a little too late. Blind optimism was stupid and dangerous. She could try to think positively, but that couldn't temper the knowledge that reality was cold and hard.

So where did that leave her?

Brady shifted, drawing her attention from the theoretical to the physical. Brady could have his pick of pretty much any woman in the metro area. There were plenty of women who would kill, cheat and lie to change places with her at this moment, but she was the one in Brady's bed—however strangely it came to be. Brady seemed content with the arrangement, and she was settling in with an ease and comfort that disturbed her nearly as much as any long-term repercussions.

They had no plans and no promises, but there were a lot of assumptions. And for the first time in her life, the assumptions didn't bother her, but the lack of plans did. She was supposed to be a free spirit, someone who loved the moment for just what it was. *Why* did she suddenly have this urge to contemplate the future? No wonder she felt out of place in her own life; this didn't feel like *her* life anymore.

And the fact she didn't hate *that* was too disturbing to contemplate.

It would be bad luck—just asking for a jinx—to celebrate victory before the votes were even cast, but Brady privately, quietly, admitted they had this one in the bag. Taylor had run a long-shot campaign and given them a couple of shocking moments, but his numbers—which had never been too high to begin with—were completely in the toilet now.

Taylor had found his moral high ground to be a little small to stand on once both of his *very* young mistresses joined him there. The catfight had been painful to watch, but when Mistress Number One brought out a child that looked much like Taylor, Mistress Number Two topped that with proof he'd been taking bribes to award no-bid contracts while in the state legislature. The ensuing debacle caused his campaign to implode and even the most vocal antiincumbent voices had come back to the Marshall camp. With only ten days until the election, there was simply no time to contain the damage and regroup.

For all Douglas Marshall's faults and failings, Brady knew his father didn't have mistresses or corruption scandals waiting in the wings. There were many unpleasant words he could use to describe his father, but stupid wasn't one of them.

So at a time when most campaigns were in a last minute flurry of activity, Marshall HQ was remarkably calm. Aspyn had even taken the afternoon off, saying she needed to help Margo at the bookstore.

Thanks to Taylor's spectacular crash-and-burn, the

schedule for this weekend had lightened up considerably, and he was looking forward to an enjoyable, *normal* Friday evening.

Lauren sat across from him, finalizing plans for election night parties. "If I didn't know better, I'd think you'd set this whole thing up. The timing is too perfect."

"I'm not that good."

"You are, actually, and I must say, this has been one of the best-run campaigns this season. Everyone says so, and as a member of your staff, I think it's been almost flawless."

Lauren's voice was casual, but she'd worked for him too long to get away with that blatant flattery. He sighed. "Yes, you will be getting a bonus."

She smiled. "Just checking. Senator Reynold's chief of staff called me yesterday afternoon. He'd like to arrange a meeting. He's looking for some new blood for his campaign."

"That's going to be a mean one. He'll be facing a primary challenge. It's not undeserved, but it makes it even harder to gain momentum." His brain immediately began to whirr, plotting and planning...

"Should I schedule the meeting?" Lauren asked.

Two weeks ago, he would have said yes. Now, though... "Not immediately. Tell him we'll chat after the first of the year. I'm going to take a couple of weeks off after the election. There's a nice warm beach somewhere with my name on it."

"I think that's a great plan. Want me to call your travel agent? Get her to come up with some ideas?"

"Sure. Just tell Sarah to pick a place where there are no elections going on."

In the blandest, coolest voice he'd ever heard from her,

she added quietly, "And should I tell her to make the reservations for two?"

He shot a look in Lauren's direction, but she was feigning deep interest in catering orders. Somehow, though, he wasn't surprised Lauren was wise to the facts of his extraoffice time with Aspyn.

But reservations for two? The idea of a vacation had only occurred to him this morning, and he hadn't explored the idea in any depth. But now that Lauren mentioned it, he had rather assumed... Taking Aspyn seemed the natural thing to do. The idea held appeal, too. More appeal than he expected.

Election Day had always loomed large on the calendar; the time before it overcrowded and overscheduled, then nothing but emptiness beyond. He hadn't had time to think beyond that date. He did now, and he felt guilty he hadn't consciously thought about his relationship with Aspyn past that point in time, either.

But then, Aspyn didn't talk about anything past Election Day, either, so he had no idea where she stood on the issue. Aspen lived firmly in the moment, so it wasn't something he could assume she'd even thought about.

Once the polls closed on Election Day, Aspyn would no longer be a member of his staff or an employee of his family. There would be no moral, ethical or political reason *not* to take her away for a while.

But what about all those other reasons...

"Just ask Sarah for ideas of good places to go this time of year."

Lauren nodded and thankfully didn't mention the topic of Aspyn again. But it didn't stop him from thinking about it. He honestly had no idea what Aspyn would say to such an idea, and had no idea how to broach the subject.

So when Aspyn provided him an opening that evening, he had to take it. She'd gone to the kitchen for a drink and came dashing back into the bedroom, shedding his shirt and practically diving under the duvet.

"Brrr. I hate the first few days that it turns off cold. I know it's not *that* cold, but coming right out of summer, I feel like I'm suddenly living in Alaska." She snuggled up next to him and stuck cold toes under his calf to warm them. "I'll be more accepting by February, but right now, I just want to be warm. Like on-a-beach-in-Hawaii-in-the-sun warm."

"I was having similar tropical thoughts today. Not because of the cold, but wanting to get away for a while after the election."

"You should. You've been going almost nonstop. You deserve some R and R." She tucked the duvet around her shoulders. "A few days of sand, sea and sun are exactly what you need."

"So you want to go?"

Aspyn froze, then her eyebrows pulled together and she slowly turned to face him. She looked shocked, but he couldn't tell if it was good shock or horrified shock. "The two of us? Like a vacation?"

"Well, yes. Exactly like a vacation." When Aspyn didn't say anything, an unfamiliar feeling crept over him. He vaguely identified it as disappointment. Until now, he hadn't realized how much the idea had grown on him.

Belatedly he realized that *she* had grown on him as well, and the disappointment had a one-two punch.

"Are you sure about that, Brady?"

"We're talking a couple of weeks, not a permanent move. And if I wasn't sure, I wouldn't have brought it up."

Aspyn's face lit up. "Then, *yes*, I'd love to go with you."

"Where do you want to go? Hawaii? Belize? The Maldives?"

"Sure." She crawled on top of him, fitting herself against his body as it stirred to life. "I assume it will be somewhat secluded? Where bathing suits can be optional?"

"I do like my privacy." He let his hands roam over her back and cupped them around the soft flesh of her butt.

"Wow, I'm feeling warmer already," she said and sat up, letting the duvet slide off her shoulders and puddle on his legs.

He let his hands trace over her waist and ribs, and ran his fingers over the curve of her breasts. Aspyn's eyes closed as he teased her nipples to hard points, and her breath grew shallow. "You look hot."

She grinned and rocked her pelvis gently against his. He flipped her to her back and pinned her to the mattress with a kiss.

"I should warn you, I'm thinking ten miles from any-where." He slid down her body, letting his tongue trace a line from her neck to her navel. Aspyn lifted her hips when he moved to her inner thigh, her hands already kneading the sheets in anticipation. "So we'll have to come up with ways to entertain each other."

The heat and movement of Brady's tongue was a mag-ical thing, and Aspyn bit back a shout at the first slow, torturous lick. Her hands fisted and her back arched as Brady's determined and unhurried pace carried her to the brink and held her there until she screamed and couldn't control the tremors racking her body. Just when Aspyn thought she couldn't take another second, Brady slipped a finger inside her and pushed her over the edge.

She was still gathering the frayed shreds of her sanity as Brady knelt between her thighs and drove home. The rising force of another orgasm, so quickly on the heels of the first, had her gasping and seeing starbursts. And as she reached the summit again, she never wanted it to end.

But it wasn't until she was nearly asleep in Brady's arms that she realized she never wanted *any* of it to end.

CHAPTER EIGHT

ASPYN had no idea where the Maldives were, but she wanted to go. While she knew Brady was a man of action, she hadn't realized that the vacation of last night's invitation was already in the works. Brady had left her on the couch with a cup of coffee and his laptop while he went to shower, telling her to look at the information his travel agent sent over and pick where she wanted to go.

Five seconds after she clicked through on the first link, her decision was made. It looked like paradise, a real heaven on earth, and from the website, the resort was determined to preserve their beautiful scenery with environmentally friendly policies to minimize their impact. Luxurious *and* responsible. She loved this place already.

As she sipped her coffee, she wondered if Brady had told his travel agent to check into the eco-policies of possible destinations or if that was just a coincidence. If it had been intentional, that would mean Brady had planned to ask her to come with him *before* last night. And if that wasn't enough to put a happy, fuzzy feeling in her chest, the knowledge that Brady understood her enough to know *that* would be important to her really made the happy-fuzzies fill her.

Though she was sold, she figured she should at least

look at some of the other options in case that wasn't
Brady's first choice and they needed to compromise. In
the next room, the hum of Brady's electric razor fell quiet
and the rush of water replaced it. She had the urge to go
join him in the shower, but she controlled it. She closed
the email about the Maldives and scrolled down to the next
one from his travel agent. That subject line was "Kauai,
Hawaii."

Choices, choices.

Before she could open it, though, she noticed her name
in the return address field three emails below that. That
would be her last report, one she was quite proud of in
that she'd managed to actually organize all the comments
in such a way as to get some actual statistical data from
it. She wished she'd paid a bit more attention in college
when they'd covered data compilation and analysis, because she'd sweated blood getting that together. She'd
wanted to talk to Brady about the trends she'd discovered
and get his input on what that might mean, but she kept
getting distracted.

Laughing to herself, she shifted in her seat as she
thought about how good Brady was at distracting her from
pretty much everything that wasn't him.

Then she noticed it was still marked as "unread."
Strange. She'd sent that days ago; he'd had plenty of time
to read it. And not only was it unread, but it hadn't been
forwarded yet to the senator's aide. Even if Brady *had* been
too busy to read it, surely he would have sent it on anyway.
Her reports were supposed to go in twice a week, and if
he hadn't sent it yet, the report was late.

She didn't want anyone in the senator's office to think
she was slacking off. Her personal life was eating up more
of her time these days, but she was still on top of what she

was doing. When or if people found out she and Brady had extracurricular activities going on, she didn't want them to be able to say she'd let that affect her work ethic.

Her idea to send it directly to the senator's office instead of via Brady had been shot down, but if Brady had forgotten, she would *still* be the one blamed and looking bad in the end. It was just one of the many things she'd learned recently about politics: who was at fault was less important than who could be blamed, and blame was doled out liberally when things went wrong. And the most blame always landed at the bottom of the flow chart.

Once he got out of the shower, she'd tell him and get him to forward it today with an explanation. Senator Marshall's aides wouldn't get it until Monday morning, but at least it would be in.

She could strangle Brady for this. Peeved, but not truly angry, she closed out the email client with the intention of checking her own email quickly. But once she closed that window, a folder on Brady's desktop caught her eye.

Breedlove, M.A.

Confused, Aspyn looked at the names of the other folders on the laptop. None of the other staffers had a whole file on Brady's computer. That bad feeling she hadn't felt in a while crept back up her spine. Something wasn't right.

She dithered. Opening the file would be snooping, and she had no right to read anything on Brady's computer. It would be wrong to do so. An invasion of his privacy. A breech in protocol.

But the folder did have her name on it, so didn't she have the right to look at something that was obviously about her? It wasn't like she could learn something confidential about herself. Even the most confidential files should be open to the persons concerned. Wasn't that a law or something?

She'd never snooped. Not once in her life. The curiosity was killing her, but something told her she didn't want to know. Maybe she was overreacting; there was no telling what was in there. It could be strictly personal in nature.

But what kind of personal files about her would Brady make? Why would he keep them on a computer that technically belonged to the campaign? *And why would it be labeled like that instead of simply as "Aspyn"?*

Curiosity won out. She listened carefully to make sure the water was still running, then clicked on the icon.

Okay, there were all of her written reports. Brady must be keeping copies on his hard drive. *That made sense.* What didn't make sense were all the other documents labeled with her name and various dates.

The first file was her background check. The idea still irked her, but she understood better now why Brady checked people out before letting them into the circle. The Marshalls were too prominent, too rich and too connected to trust blindly. *Damn, it was thorough.* Things she'd almost forgotten—like that incident at the demonstration in West Virginia where they were protesting mining methods—were described in detail. And a look at the date in the header showed the information had been pulled together with astounding speed. Brady had access to her life story just days after she hit the news.

Oddly, the background check had been done through his family's business, not the campaign or the senator's office, and that seemed off.

As did the information in the next document, which outlined how she'd be paid out of noncampaign funds because she wasn't a campaign employee.

With alarm bells clanging in her ears, she started snooping without any remorse or hesitation at all. That bad feeling she'd been ignoring had been trying to tell her something, and as she opened document after document inside her little folder, it became clear exactly what it had been trying to say.

She was an idiot. A fool.

And Brady Marshall was a lying snake.

As Brady got out of the shower, he could hear Aspyn in the bedroom moving around. "That didn't take long," he called as he dried off. "Did you come to a decision?"

"You're damn right I did." She punctuated the statement with a door slamming shut.

He wrapped a towel around his waist and entered the bedroom. Aspyn was dressed—albeit rather haphazardly as her shirt was buttoned wrong—and was loading the few personal items she'd started keeping here into her overnight bag. She pushed past him into the bathroom and grabbed her toiletries.

He blocked her exit, wanting to know what was going on. "We can't actually leave until after the election," he teased. "Don't you think it's a bit early to be packing?"

"I'm sure you'll have a fantastic time. Now," she said through gritted teeth, "get out of my way."

He'd never seen Aspyn this angry about anything. Color flagged her cheeks and unshed tears glistened in her eyes. She could get peevish about things, but right now he was lucky looks couldn't kill. "What did I miss?" he said to her back as she ducked around him.

"*You* didn't miss anything. You're right on the ball as always. *I'm* the one who's getting caught up. And now that I understand what's really going on…" She stopped and took a deep breath, but her jaw and shoulders stayed tense. "I'm going home."

Responding in kind wouldn't help the situation any. He tried to keep his voice light. "That much I picked up on. Can I ask why?"

"And *again* with the patronizing." She shoved her arms through a cardigan and pulled it tight over her chest. "I really thought it was just an annoying habit of yours, but now I see it's genuine." Aspyn grabbed her bag and stomped out.

He quickly pulled on a pair of jeans and grabbed a shirt before following her. "At least tell me what happened in the last twenty minutes that's got you so mad."

Aspyn faced him, arms crossed and eyebrows raised to her hairline. "So that you can reduce the negative impact and channel the sentiment into a controlled, positive message?"

Where had he heard that before? He glanced at the couch and saw his laptop. *Oh, sh—*

"I see we're on the same page now. Good. We can quit pretending that what comes out of your mouth is anything other than a big, fat—"

"Aspyn, calm down."

Her eyes grew wide. "You think that's possible? You *lied*, Brady. To me, to the press…hell, to everyone outside your little political spin machine. I knew there was something fishy going on, but I let you convince me that you and your father and his staff actually gave a damn about anything other than getting reelected and keeping that Senate seat in the family."

Brady straightened his shoulders. That was a cheap shot. "We do."

"Only about the detrimental impact on the campaign if

word gets out that you don't. You don't care what I or anyone else thinks is important. You played me *and* the people you claim to represent. You let us think you really wanted to listen, but I might as well be shouting into a hole in the ground." She shook her head, her disappointment and frustration clearly on display. "I was nothing but a shiny object to catch everyone's attention and deflect anything real."

He chose his words carefully. "You're partly right. I won't lie to you about that."

"What a refreshing change."

He ignored the sarcasm. "Our immediate priority was to quell the uprising, and, if possible, channel that into something good for our image. That's smart politics, and you were the key to that. There's a lot that went on behind the scenes that you didn't see, but we have to keep the bigger picture in mind when we—"

"Oh, screw your 'big picture.' I'm so tired of hearing about it. 'Big picture' is nothing more than a nice way to say that the ends justify the means. They don't. It's immoral and it's wrong to lie and use people."

"No one's used you, Aspyn." He stepped toward her, but she backed away. He tried to appeal to her rationality. "I told you to temper your expectations, that nothing you were doing would have immediate impact. I'm sorry if that hurts your feelings, but you were hired to do a job and that job was made clear to you, to the press and the people. Anything you inferred beyond that isn't my fault."

"What a convenient and nice salve for your conscience." She shot him a look that clearly said he wasn't going to like what came next. "So where exactly did sleeping with me come into this? Was that part of the plan from the beginning? Or did you just decide later it would be a good way to distract me and cause me to focus on you instead of this so-called job?"

"That's not—"

"You know what, Brady?" She reached under the coffee table for her shoes and rammed her feet inside. "The sad thing is that I almost respect how you handled 'Aspyn, The Campaign Headache.' That's how much being involved with politics, even for a short time, has twisted my thinking. I actually understand being used in that way and that makes me disgusted with myself. What I can't get over is that you could lie to me and still have sex with me. And even worse, lie to me about what that sex meant. That's even more disgusting, and I can't find any reason to respect it."

She fished her keys out of her bag and removed the clip holding his door keys from the ring. She tossed it on the table, the clatter overly loud in the heavy silence. Hauling her bag over her shoulder, she grabbed her coat and turned to face him. "You'll find my letter of resignation on your hard drive, filed in the appropriate folder."

She headed for the door, head held high and shoulders stiff. He trailed behind. "Wait. You get to throw all that out there, but I don't get the chance to respond?"

"Mmm-hmm. There's really nothing left to say."

"I disagree." He grabbed her arm.

She twisted free and glared at him. "Tough."

He prayed for patience. "Aspyn, can you wait just one second and let me—"

"No." She didn't break stride or pause as she wrenched the door open. "You are the last person on earth I want to listen to."

Her words still hung in the air as the door closed behind her with a bang. Brady felt drained and off balance, like he'd just ridden out a hurricane and didn't know where to start with the recovery efforts.

He should be angry Aspyn had nosed through his computer files without permission, but in her shoes, he probably would have done the same thing. He was the one who gave her use of his laptop to begin with, so he couldn't complain too much she'd found something she wasn't meant to see.

Aspyn had the right facts, but her interpretation was wrong. Mostly. Well, partly.

In reality, Aspyn's true purpose for being at HQ had quit being important to him a while ago. Eventually he'd have thought to explain the realities of the situation to her, but he'd moved past that before "eventually" ever arrived.

And now she felt betrayed. By him. Old anger at his father stirred in his belly. Once again, his father's sins were lumped on him to pay for. He deserved a little condemnation for participation in this debacle, but the fault came from the top.

What really sucked was Aspyn's jump from professional to personal and the sordid way she tied them together. No wonder she claimed disgust. When viewed through that lens, it was tawdry and disgusting. But he'd never connected the two spheres as she had.

That required a baffling leap of logic he simply wasn't capable of making and an equally large amount of overreaction.

The drip of water onto his shoulder sent him back to the bedroom in search of his towel. As he scrubbed it over his hair, he remembered Aspyn's remark about her resignation letter.

He hadn't been in the shower all that long. Aspyn had to have worked fast to get from snooping through his computer files to jumping to conclusions to writing a resignation letter *and* getting packed.

Curious, he clicked on Aspyn's folder and searched the file names. There it was, properly marked "Breedlove, M.A., Resignation Letter," and today's date.

To: Brady Marshall, Marshall For Senate Campaign
From: Aspyn Breedlove
RE: I quit.
Since I cannot, in reality, resign from a nonexistent position that I never actually held, this letter seems redundant and unnecessary. However, I feel it is important to officially state my separation from a morally questionable work environment—a decision made immediately upon my discovery of the repugnant truth behind the story of my brief time with this campaign. I hold myself to higher ethical standards than demonstrated in this campaign and cannot continue in a situation that may damage my reputation by association.

Aspyn *had* learned a lot from her brief affair with politics. She'd removed herself from the situation *and* done so in a way that cleared her of complicity. She was good. Adept at the game.

She'd calm down. She said she understood their motives behind hiring her, and once she had time to get past the shock and hurt feelings, Aspyn would be more open to discussion about the personal aspect.

He just didn't know how long it would take her to get to that point.

I will not mope. Things end. I knew it would.

Aspyn scrubbed the grout around her bathtub with

renewed—if somewhat forced—energy. Oh, she was still mad; the righteous indignation of this debacle could carry her for a long time.

She'd explained her arrival this morning to Margo with just an "I think I'm coming down with something," and locked herself in her apartment. Margo, of course, had brought up a cup of something warm and vile-smelling shortly thereafter. But the older woman had taken a close look at her, said she looked terrible and told Aspyn to go to bed and stay there. A look in the mirror confirmed it: she looked as bad as she felt.

And therein lay the problem. She didn't just feel mad; there was hurt and anger totally unrelated to Brady's lies about her job with the campaign in there, too.

That made everything worse because she shouldn't be hurt. She should just be angry. Angry about being used, regardless of how and why. The fact she was hurt only made her more angry—mainly at herself for letting her get into a position where Brady could hurt her at all.

The fact she *wanted* to mope about him made her even angrier at herself.

Scrubbing grout was punishment for those sins as well as an outlet for her anger.

Be angry. Not hurt.

Being hurt brought up all kinds of issues she really didn't want to face. Self-examination of her feelings didn't seem like a good idea right now. She might not like what she discovered.

Aspyn had a sneaking suspicion that she knew what lay beneath, but avoidance meant she wouldn't have to really face it yet. Denial was her friend right now. Eventually she'd have enough distance to reflect, learn and grow from the experience.

Working for the Marshall campaign had been an aberration from the norm, but sleeping with Brady Marshall had been a dip into insanity. It was a *good* thing she'd found out the truth about both situations before anything got out of hand. She was *lucky* to escape from that whole political scene and the people in it unscathed.

Oh, who am I kidding? I'm totally scathed.

She sat back against the bathroom wall and leaned her head against the cool tile. It was disgusting. She was caught: hook, line and sinker. Oh, she talked a good game, but she'd been sucked all the way in by Brady.

Brady Marshall: everything she should never want in a man. He wore ties and belonged to the country club, owned horses and played golf. *Golf,* the *most* ridiculous and useless sport ever. Brady benefited from the status quo, excelled in the system. One person who was such her polar opposite they might as well be different species.

Goddess help her, she'd fallen in love with the jerk.

"Where's Aspyn? She said she'd help with the invitations."

Brady just happened to be standing there checking his schedule with Lauren when one of the volunteers stuffing election-night party invitations into envelopes asked the question.

"Aspyn resigned from the campaign," Lauren answered without a pause.

There was a group gasp, followed by a moment of shocked silence as the volunteers looked at each other.

Mrs. Jackson, an elderly grandmother type who'd volunteered for Marshall campaigns since his grandfather's second term, looked at Lauren in disbelief. "She quit? A week before the election?"

Lauren was the only person he'd told, and only after

Aspyn hadn't shown up this morning. He'd been working under the assumption that once she cooled down, she'd regret her resignation and show up like nothing had happened. So much for his assumptions.

He certainly didn't think Aspyn's absence would be a big deal at HQ and hadn't seen the sense in an announcement. Maybe he should have let Lauren say something official to everyone. She had the ability and aplomb to treat this like she would for any other employee—something he was discovering he lacked. Lauren, though, regrouped well. "She tendered her letter of resignation Saturday."

"But why?" another volunteer he vaguely recognized asked.

Lauren shrugged. "Personal reasons."

"Bless her heart." Murmurs of agreement rumbled around the table, with an "Oh, dear, how terrible" tossed in as well.

Aspyn wasn't dead, she just quit—not that someone would realize that from the reactions here. "I'm sure Aspyn's just fine," he said to quell the dismay.

Mrs. Jackson frowned at him. "Aspyn's worked so hard and she loved it here so much. To resign this close to the finish line… It would have to be something bad."

No, just a morally questionable work environment. And a boss she thinks is a liar and a user.

"That's not the impression she gave me." He should have saved his breath. The conversation went on around the table like he hadn't commented at all.

"Has anyone talked to her? I hope she knows we're here if she needs us."

"I just hope nothing happened to her parents."

"Should we could call Margo? She would know what's going on."

"I'm sending her an email right now."

Brady walked away—not that anyone noticed his departure. They were all too busy taking up a collection for a basket of mini-muffins to send to her apartment.

He hadn't realized she'd made so many friends around here. On second thought, though, it wasn't that much of a surprise. She'd gotten off to a rocky start, but after that, she'd made a place for herself here. He just hadn't realized how deeply she'd settled in and made herself at home.

Which made her ongoing silence all the more frustrating. He'd called her Saturday night, but she hadn't answered and still hadn't returned his call. Not only was she angry, but she was nursing that anger. He never would have pegged Aspyn as the kind to carry a grudge.

It bothered him a lot more than it should. First, it was insulting to think Aspyn believed he would take her to bed with some ulterior motive. She could castigate him all day long for the not-entirely-honest representation of her position with the campaign and he'd suffer it. But he wasn't low enough to use her—or anyone—just for his own sexual gratification or this election. Did she really think he was that much of a lowlife?

He hadn't slept well last night; the bed felt too empty. He had no problem sleeping alone—never had—so it wasn't just the fact Aspyn wasn't there. No, her continued silence had a part of him worried that Aspyn would never be there again.

Which was completely ridiculous. It had only been forty-eight hours since she stormed out. Maybe her temper needed longer than that to cool down. And even if she was determined to never speak to him again, why was he so bothered about it? She'd told him up-front this was only short-term. Their definitions of short-term just differed, that's all.

Aspyn had been a nice distraction, an interesting break from the norm and the routine. Things could go back to normal now.

But, damn it, normal wasn't remotely interesting right now. It was dull and boring and predictable. Right or wrong, he had a need to see Aspyn.

And *that* bothered him a lot.

CHAPTER NINE

"HERE, honey. I brought you a drink." Margo hadn't even waited for Aspyn to tell her to come in before she was barging through the door.

Aspyn pulled the afghan up tighter around her chest and muted the sound on the TV. Much to her everlasting shame, she was now in a full-out moping funk.

"Thanks, Margo, but I'm—"

"No buts." Margo pressed the cup into her hand. It was cool, not hot, and when Aspyn lifted it to her nose for a sniff, the alcohol fumes nearly singed her eyebrows.

"What *is* this?"

"That, dearie, is from my secret stash of the best moonshine ever made."

Aspyn took a tiny sip and it burned a path down to her stomach. "Wow."

"Sip slowly. It'll sneak up on you."

The second sip was easier. "So, what's the occasion?"

Margo's face was kind and sympathetic without crossing into pity. "I think you're far past any herbal remedy's ability to help. I thought the 'shine might be more appropriate."

Lovely. "Is it that obvious?"

Margo nudged Aspyn's feet until she curled them up

and made space on the futon for Margo to join her. "You haven't left your apartment in days. So, yeah, it's that obvious."

Aspyn groaned and closed her eyes. "I'm pathetic, aren't I?"

"No, honey, you're heartbroken. I know that's probably a first for you, but there's still no shame in it."

There was no sense denying it or pretending her heart wasn't involved. "Oh, there's plenty of shame. Some embarrassment, a little self-loathing and a lot of disappointment are mixed in there, too, but it's all still shameful."

"He's a handsome, charming guy. Any girl could lose her head. Or her heart."

"It's ridiculous. I shouldn't have lost anything at all." She gave Margo the abbreviated version of this mess. "I was able to keep the job and the sex separate. Or at least I thought I was doing a good job of that. But now it's all tangled up together."

"And Brady?"

"I wasn't supposed to get emotionally attached to him and now I feel used. Even worse? He used me to fool other people. I'm complicit in perpetuating a deception on people. Just another pawn in the game." The moonshine was going down easier now and had kindled a nice warm glow in her stomach. It felt good. In fact, she felt better all over.

"Then call him out. I still have the business cards from a dozen of those reporters. I'm sure any of them would love to tell this story."

"To what end? Right now, my shame is at least somewhat private."

"It would expose Brady and his father as manipulators."

"'Politicians Lie' isn't exactly headline news." She snorted. "Not in this town. At most, it might embarrass

Brady a little. All he really cares about is the election and this wouldn't even make a ripple there." She thought for a minute, tracing her finger around the rim of the cup. "No, whining to the press wouldn't solve anything and would only make me look petty. In fact, it would probably be worse for me. I'm going to look like the bimbo trying to get her hooks into the Marshall Empire. I'll be the punch line to a joke."

Margo frowned. "The Marshalls lied to you and to everyone. With the right spin, you could do *some* damage."

Aspyn sipped at her drink and thought about that for a minute. "I guess."

"But…?"

"But I don't hate him enough to do something like that. And the family—other than his father—doesn't really deserve it, either."

"Oh, honey." Margo patted her leg. "You really do love him."

She groaned. "Yes, as stupid as that is."

"Loving someone is never stupid. Love makes you do stupid, crazy things sometimes, but it isn't stupid."

"Me being in love with Brady Marshall is stupid."

"Why, honey?"

Let me count the ways. "We're just too different."

"I don't know about that," Margo said with a shrug. "You seemed to get along okay up to now. Maybe your differences are good for each other. It allows you both to grow as people."

"In *our* world, maybe that's okay. But not in Brady's."

Margo frowned. "Last time I checked, we were all on the same planet."

"Brady can't be involved with someone like me." Her

voice dropped a smidge into the pathetic range. "Not publicly."

"You make it sound like there's something wrong with you, and I assure you, there's not."

"Brady needs…" The moonshine was making it hard to put things into words properly—even if she could make her tongue work properly. "He needs a specific kind of woman. A Jackie Kennedy to stand beside him and look the part while he rules the world."

"So you *were* thinking long-term for once."

Ouch. "No! Maybe? Damn, that's even crazier. I mean, can you see me in a little pillbox hat?"

"I think you'd look adorable in a pillbox hat. I wish they were still in style. Maybe we could try to bring them back."

"Focus, Margo. Please."

"Sorry." She cleared her throat. "I think we never know what we really need until Fate gives it to us. You and Brady might be—"

"Disastrous?"

"I was leaning toward 'balancing.' When did you get so cynical?"

"It's very easy to be cynical once you understand how things actually work in this world. Everyone is just shouting at the storm and it doesn't make any difference." She sighed. "You can't restack the deck."

Margo's eyes widened. "Mercy. No wonder the energy in here is terrible. I'll bring up some carnelian and topaz crystals to clear out some of this pessimism."

"I'm learning pessimism isn't always a bad thing. It's healthy. What's dangerous is optimism."

"You are in worse shape than I thought. And this—" she took the cup out of Aspyn's hand "—isn't helping." She stood and tugged Aspyn to her feet. "We're going down-stairs."

Aspyn had to fight to keep her balance on rubbery legs and feet that felt farther away than normal. "Margo, I don't want tea and my chakras are aligned and functioning. My aura is fine—if a little tipsy," she added. "I appreciate the thought, but I just want to mope a while longer."

Margo cupped a hand around her cheek and smiled sup-portively. "Okay. But only until morning. That's the maxi-mum amount of moping anyone is allowed. Tomorrow we cleanse and move on. You're too good for this."

"Thanks, Margo." Glad Margo was taking the moon-shine with her, Aspyn collapsed back onto the futon and the room swam at the edges.

"But let me give you one more thing to think about. Jackie Kennedy was one strong lady who did some good things while wearing that pillbox hat. It's not an all-or-nothing proposition."

"That's a sellout."

"Goodness, no. Conformity can be deceptive. No one ever watches for the attack to come from the inside. Even if you're not willing to forgive Brady, at least forgive your-self. And think about what the universe wanted you to learn from this lesson."

Back under the afghan, Aspyn did just that as she slowly sobered up. She'd been so caught up in her private misery, she'd forgotten her original plans. She *had* gotten some-thing out of this.

And just as she could apply what she'd learned about politics to her professional life, Brady would have to be a learning experience for her private life. In the future, she'd be more careful about who she let into her heart and mind. She'd been too easily seduced, too willing to trust and accept without questions. She'd been stupid and naïve, ignoring her instincts and letting herself be guided by something other than her intellect and common sense.

Growth never came easy. And it hurt like she couldn't believe. But she could be stronger for the experience.

Eventually.

Just a few more days and this election would be in the history books. He should be happy, enjoying the wave of good press and poll numbers, congratulating himself on a job well done. But he wasn't. He was just going through the motions, shaking hands and playing his part, but the pleasure of the campaign and its success had dissipated with Aspyn's continued silence.

It wasn't like he expected Aspyn to be a permanent fixture in his life, but he hadn't realized how much he'd miss her until she'd shut him out. The look on her face when she left still haunted him.

Brady gave himself a strong mental shake as he parked behind HQ. He had to snap out of it. Nana did not tolerate tardiness, and he still had a forty-minute drive to Hill Chase ahead of him. Stopping by here might make him a few minutes late, but he could smooth that over with the Grands by telling them he'd spend a few days out there next week.

It wasn't like he had other postelection plans now.

He was sending a text to Ethan, asking him to stall, as he rounded the corner in time to see Aspyn leaving the building. His first thought caused his heart to beat for the first time in days, but that faded as he noticed the small box she carried. Her coffee mug peeked out the top, and he knew that box contained the few personal items she'd brought to liven up her work space. She hadn't come to see him; she'd come to clean out her desk. There was a finality to that somehow.

She stopped and acknowledged him with simply, "Brady."

"Good to see you, Aspyn. You look...good." In reality, she looked a little tired and shuttered, her normal radiance muted. But from the multicolored knit hat to the battered fuzzy boots on her feet, she was still quintessentially Aspyn. She even jangled slightly as she shifted the box in her arms and adjusted her jacket against the brisk wind that kicked up. "I tried to call you."

"I know." Her eyes wouldn't meet his.

"Would you like to get a cup of coffee? Go somewhere and talk?"

That finally brought her eyes to his face. "No. I just came to get my stuff and thank everyone for the muffins. I need to—"

He reached for her, but she stepped away. He put his hands in his pockets instead. "I really need to explain—"

"Brady, I don't really care what you need. It's harsh and I hate it for you, but that's the truth. I've said all I want to say and I'm not willing to listen to you justify your actions, so there's no point in dragging this out."

Anger sparked inside him. "Be reasonable, Aspyn."

Color bloomed in her cheeks as her eyes narrowed. "I don't want to be reasonable. I don't *have* to be reasonable. You lied to me. You hurt me, and I'm not over that yet. I can't believe you'd think I would be." He could hear the betrayal behind the anger in her voice, and her face hardened as she looked him over. "You're not the person I thought you were, and I don't like the person you actually are. And, more importantly, I don't like the person I was becoming because of you."

She might as well have slapped him. In fact, he would have preferred she had.

"Goodbye, Brady." Aspyn pushed past him, not quite breaking into a run, but definitely moving quickly.

A flash of movement to his right caught his attention, and he turned to see most of the campaign staff and volunteers standing near the big windows. They moved away quickly once he turned, but no doubt they'd seen everything. Depending on what Aspyn had told them about her sudden resignation, they probably had enough pieces to know what was going on.

He turned on his heel and went back to his car.

Dinner was a small, family affair and, as expected, Nana was placated for his tardiness by his intention to come out next week and stay for a while. The election gave him an easy excuse for his distractedness, and the need to get back to the city a good reason to not linger over coffee. The truth, though, was, as always, Aspyn. His temper hadn't quite cooled, and anger wasn't a good mix with everything else she stirred up in him. He really wasn't in the mood for people at all right now.

A ride would help, but he didn't have the time. But he made his way to the stable anyway for a quick visit with Spider before he drove back to the city.

The sounds and smells of the Marshall stable were familiar and comforting. Big heads popped over stall doors as he entered, and he heard Spider's whinny of recognition. "Hey, boy," he greeted the stallion. "How's things?"

Somehow, he wasn't surprised when a female voice answered. "He's going to be disappointed if you don't take him out." Lily walked around the corner from the direction of the office. Although she was Ethan's fiancée now, not too long ago she'd been an employee of the stable and was still more comfortable out here than up at the main house. She'd sat through dinner, but excused herself immediately after dessert. Everyone assumed the stable would be her destination. She still loved the horses. "You can't tease him like that."

He fed Spider a treat and rubbed his nose. "That will have to do until I get back next week."

"You know, I always meant to ask you how you came up with the name Spider for a horse."

"Finn named him, actually." Lily looked surprised. "His legs were so long when he was born, Finn said he looked more like a big black spider than a horse. It just stuck."

"Interesting." Lily reached over and gave Spider a pat.

"Make Ethan tell you how he came up with Tinker's name."

"I'll do that." At the sound of his name, Ethan's horse whinnied for attention. Lily patted him fondly. "And by the way, congrats on a well-run campaign. Good job."

"It's not over just yet, but thanks."

Lily turned like she was going to leave, but she hesitated, her eyebrows pulling together as she dithered.

He shouldn't ask and a month ago he wouldn't have, but Aspyn had had a greater effect on him than he wanted to admit. "Something on your mind, Lily?"

She shoved her hands in the pockets of her jacket. "I know it's not my business, but Ethan told me about what happened between you and Aspyn."

So much for the sanctity of brotherly talk over good whiskey. "My brother has a big mouth."

"That's very true. But since he spilled all my deep dark secrets to you, I guess we're even." She frowned. "Aspyn seems like a neat person. I'm sorry things didn't work out for either of you."

What, exactly, had Ethan told her? It might help if he could fully remember everything he'd told Ethan. His hangover from that night was something from a college nightmare. "Thanks." *That should be a safe enough comment.*

Lily opened her mouth to say something then changed her mind and closed it, shaking her head the whole time. Then she took a deep breath and blew it out. "I'm just going to risk it."

"Risk what?"

"Your wrath. What you did to Aspyn sucks."

Great. Another woman who sees this as all his fault. "I didn't 'do' anything to her. She may have misunderstood the situation, but that's not my fault."

"It never is with you Marshall boys," Lily snapped before she caught herself and cleared her throat. "You've lived in your bubble for so long, you just can't see outside it. It's a blindness for your entire family. I know it's not intentional, but it's there."

He hadn't wanted to be lectured by Ethan, and he definitely didn't want to be lectured by Lily. But he couldn't dismiss her unless he wanted Ethan coming after him for upsetting her again. "Your point?"

"My point is simple." She leaned against Tinker's stall, easily brushing the horse away when he tried to chew on her ponytail. "Take an idealistic, optimistic believer, tell her what she's hoping to hear and give her the opportunity she's been waiting for. She's going to believe it, adopt it as her own and live it wholeheartedly, because she wants to believe in the goodness and the possibilities. That's who Aspyn is."

Lily had Aspyn pegged. And that clear insight into Aspyn's psyche made him a little wary of what was still to come from Lily.

"Now you know how Ethan is about honesty. That's a direct result of this weird political bubble y'all live in. He distrusts everything until it's proven otherwise. Aspyn is the flip side of that—believing everything—but just like Ethan, she can't really see the gray area."

Lily had a good point there.

"You lied to her, Brady. You might see it as a little white lie, but Aspyn isn't going to make that distinction. Not about something like this. That one lie brings down everything she'd put belief in." She leveled a look at him. "You know I speak from experience, and you know I'm right. Oddly enough, you and I are a lot alike. We understand that gray area between totally right and totally wrong."

He nodded. "The bigger picture."

"Exactly. Ethan and Aspyn, bless their hearts, don't always see it." A small smile crossed her face. "Ethan's getting better at it these days, but Aspyn... This is probably the first time she's had that kind of slap-in-the-face betrayal of something she believed to be true."

Damn it. Lily was right. It wasn't just a lie; it was an assault against Aspyn's entire worldview. "I stomped her optimism."

"Yep. And there's no good way to recover from that. For either of you. Then there's..." Lily cut her eyes at him. "Then there's the fact you...um...expanded to a physical relationship. That makes the betrayal deeper because sex means something."

"Aspyn would disagree about that."

"She might, but I'd argue otherwise. Aspyn definitely cares for you." He swallowed his shock, and if Lily noticed, she didn't comment. "How deeply she cares, I can't say. But even if she didn't, 'Free Love' isn't empty or void of all meaning. By its nature, it's honest. And even if she didn't expect you to be a forever guy, I guarantee you she at least expected honesty in bed. If you lied to her about one thing important to her…"

He held up a hand. "I get it, Lily." He'd been flogged enough.

"Good." She looked at him. "I mean, I'm sorry that things worked out like that, but I'm glad you can see it from her perspective."

They left the stable and started to walk back up to the main house in silence. After a minute, he couldn't hold the question back any longer. "So no advice on how to fix this?"

Lily's eyebrows arched up. "I didn't know you wanted to."

Did he? "Well, *if* I wanted to, what would you suggest?"

"Well, you can't fix it and you can't make it up to her. That idea is a lie perpetrated by bad movies. What's done is done. You can't 'unhurt' someone, and she might not be willing to get past it."

"Have you always been such a pessimist?"

"I'm actually an optimist. I wouldn't be here today if I weren't. Thing is, I know you can't change the past. The only thing you can do is admit your mistakes and do better in the future." She shrugged.

"That's it? That's all you have?"

"That depends."

"On…" he prompted.

She stopped and sized him up. "Do you love her?"

He shifted his weight, uncomfortable under her stare, and she laughed. "You don't have to answer that. But you should probably plan on some serious groveling." She started walking again. "You can't jerk her around, though. Only grovel if you mean it and plan to follow through."

Before he could ask her what she meant, Ethan called her name from halfway up the path. "Lily! You ready?"

"On my way," she answered before turning back to him. "But let me know if you do decide to grovel. I wanna watch." She smirked, then she ran up the path and into his brother's arms for a big kiss.

Lily was sharper than he'd given her credit for, even if that insight wasn't all that pleasant for him at the moment.

Aspyn had invested herself in the campaign one hundred percent. She'd done everything asked of her and more, and she'd proven she had a sharp and savvy political mind. He'd originally admired her passion and commitment to her beliefs, and she deserved the honest chance he'd implied she had. That much he could easily do. He could make amends for that part of the problem.

As for Aspyn herself...

Did he love her?

He missed her. He worried about her. He was angry at himself for hurting her, and angry at her for not returning his calls. Aspyn was the one person who never bored him, the one person who could surprise him.

She made him eat quiche and tofu and worry about the rain forests. She made him feel optimistic about the future. And he could easily see her in *his* future, now that he could admit his view of the future had changed because of her.

Damn.

It was a bit disconcerting to Aspyn how quickly her life went back to normal. Even more disconcerting was how no one seemed to find it odd that she'd left the campaign this close to the election.

No, the *most* disconcerting thing was how few people even noticed at all. *Talk about a flash in the pan.* Society as a whole, Aspyn decided, had the attention span of a goldfish. After all the hoopla about getting their politicians to listen to them, no one seemed to realize or care that her return to her old life meant no one was listening to them now.

No wonder pessimism and cynicism reigned supreme on Capitol Hill.

And with her current attitude, she'd fit right in. *Ugh*.

She ripped the credit card receipt off the roll and handed it and the stack of books to the man on the other side of the counter. From her bag tucked away near her feet, she heard her phone ring and dug it out as the door closed behind him.

"Aspyn Breedlove?"

"Speaking."

"This is Kelly James in Senator Peters's office."

Aspyn swallowed hard. Senator Peters was a ranking member on the Committee on Environment and Public Works. *Whoa*. She tried to ignore the pump of adrenaline into her system. *She probably thinks I'm still with the campaign or something.* "Yes, how can I help you?"

"Senator Marshall's office sent over some of the data and reports you worked on for them."

"They *did*?" she squeaked. She cleared her throat and tried again. "Really?"

"I must admit some of the trends you note are quite intriguing, but I'm also interested in a footnote you have here referring to…"

Aspyn had to sit. An aide to one of the most powerful

men in the Senate when it came to environmental policy had read her report. Margo rushed over, concern written all over her face, but Aspyn waved her away. "I'd be happy to provide the source material for you."

"Wonderful. Could we set up a short meeting for sometime next week?"

Aspyn's world swayed slightly and she nearly fell off the stool. "Next week? Sure. I'd like that."

"How's Thursday around two for you?"

Margo slipped something in my tea earlier that's causing me to hallucinate. "That would be great."

"I'm going to email you a few things to look at and a couple of other questions your data raises…"

Nope. This was real. Aspyn jumped up and did a happy dance as Kelly confirmed her email address and said goodbye. After making sure the call was disconnected, she grabbed Margo in a huge hug. "Yay! This is amazing!"

"I'm so happy for you, honey. What's amazing?"

"I've got a meeting with an aide in Senator Peters's office next week."

"I have no idea what that means, but I'm thrilled for you nonetheless." Margo squeezed her shoulders tight.

"Well, I know *exactly* what that means."

Aspyn whirled around at the amused voice. "Mom!" She ran and was caught in a hug that smelled of sandalwood and vanilla—the two scents she always associated with her parents. "What are you doing back? Where's Dad? Is everything okay?"

"He was right behind me. Who knows what's distracted him. Everything is fine, and we're here to see you, of course." Her mom gave her another squeeze, then greeted Margo.

"There's my girl."

"Dad!"

As her father hugged the breath out of her, she heard her mother say, "Allen, Aspyn has a meeting with Senator Peters's office next week."

Her dad held her at arm's length, surprise written on his face. "Is this true?"

Her heart sank to her knees. "I can explain. I swear."

"I certainly hope so," her father huffed. "I went on a hunger strike on the steps of the Capitol Building and got diddly. You get handcuffed to a senator's son, start a revolution and end up with the ear of not one, but two senators, in what? A month? That's unreal. Good for you."

She searched their faces. "You're not mad at me?"

Her mom blinked. "*Mad*? Why on earth would we be mad?"

"You are obviously a force to be reckoned with," her father added.

Aspyn had to pick her jaw up off the floor before she could speak. "Really? I am?"

Her mom led her over to Margo's couch and sat. "Goodness, what did you think?"

"I was afraid you'd think I'd sold out my principles. Gone over to the Dark Side."

Her father sat on her other side. "Did you?"

"No! But I know how you feel about—"

Her mom patted her knee. "Aspyn, you're making your waves your way. And it seems to be working for you."

"Pretty damn well, I'd say," her father added. "Maybe we should take a few pointers from you."

Pride swelled in her chest.

"I told you so," Margo added.

So did Brady. Her heart contracted painfully at the thought of him. She shouldn't be thinking about him.

"Who?" her mom asked, and she realized she'd said it aloud.

She forced herself to smile, but it felt odd and fake on her face. "Brady Marshall. The one I got handcuffed to. He's probably the one responsible for getting me the meeting with Peters's aide," she realized, and that meant she needed to have a think as to what Brady was up to now.

It would have to be later, though. Thinking about Brady hurt too much. Right now, her head was spinning in a good way, and she didn't want to ruin this moment by letting that pain out.

"So tell us about this Brady Marshall person. I remember when his grandfather was in the Senate…"

Damn.

On Tuesday, Aspyn went to the polls early. She was tempted to retaliate, and for a minute her pen hovered over the box for Mack Taylor. But she couldn't. She'd worked too hard; *everyone* at HQ had worked too hard for her to betray them by throwing away her vote out of spite and anger.

Who would ever have thought an election could make her cry.

CHAPTER TEN

MARSHALL Sweeps To A Third Term, the headlines shouted at Aspyn Wednesday morning. Not that she was all that surprised at the election results, but working on a *winning* campaign would look much better on her résumé than working on a losing one. If she ever got around to updating it, that was. At this point, she wasn't sure what she was going to do with all her new knowledge and connections, if anything at all.

It was absolutely ridiculous to let her personal feelings for Brady affect her decisions about future career options, but right now, the two were too tangled together for her to want to investigate that path.

That was why she was holding off making any decisions at all—beyond keeping that meeting next week with Kelly—until she'd had time to process and heal. She didn't want to make emotional choices she might regret later.

A picture of Brady, his father and grandfather at the victory party last night took up a fourth of the page. The caption beneath read A Family Affair, and a sidebar outlined the Marshall family's long history in politics and hinted it was a trend they expected to continue.

Brady looked happy, if a little tired. And he wasn't wearing a tie, which struck her as significant even though she knew it wasn't. *I'm losing my mind.* She flipped the paper over.

Rain splattered on the bookstore's front windows and the occasional rumble of thunder rolled overhead. It was a dreary, nasty day that matched her dreary, nasty mood— a mood made even worse by the knowledge she could be winging her way to a sunny tropical locale with Brady right now.

Let's not play the "if only" game. Life presents us with choices. We make them and live with the consequences.

The weather kept most people indoors, so the bookstore was empty except for Aspyn and one of Margo's Reiki clients waiting for Margo to finish up with the current one. Aspyn's bad mood made concentration impossible, so she grabbed her coffee cup, went to the couch next to the magazine display and pulled one at random to flip through.

The bell over the door dinged and Aspyn closed the magazine, thankful for the possibility of *something* to do. *"Namaste,"* she called out. "How can I help you…" She trailed off as she saw Brady standing on the mat, the rain dripping off his hair and coat. "Oh. Brady."

"Aspyn." He shook his head, sending water flying. His face was unreadable, giving her no clue why he was here. And she was having a really hard time coming up with a reason. *Any* reason.

Be an adult. "Is there something particular you're looking for? Cleansing crystals? Maybe a relaxation CD?"

"I'm looking for you." Her heart stuttered at the force in the statement. "It's time for us to talk."

She tidied the magazine rack, even though it didn't need it. "I've pretty much said all I have to say on the subject."

His jaw was tight. "A courtesy you haven't extended to me."

"There's nothing left to talk about."

"I disagree."

She shot a look over where Margo's client waited, the woman studiously pretending she was reading the back of an incense box. *Great. An audience.*

Aspyn forced herself to sound lighthearted. "You're right." Brady looked shocked. "I do need to thank you for contacting Senator Peters's office. I have a meeting with one of his aides next week."

"Good. Glad to hear it." His voice dropped a notch. "But that's not what I want to talk about."

She took a step closer, keeping her back to the woman. Dropping her voice to match his, she said, "Tough. I don't work for you anymore. The election is over, so there's no need for us to talk about anything. Unless, of course, you have metaphysical needs or interests the store can assist you with."

The muscle in Brady's jaw twitched. "Aspyn…"

"Aspyn?" Margo asked at the same time. She waved goodbye to the first client and motioned for the other to go back to the treatment room. Then she faced them both, the serene smile on her face telling them both to behave. "Is everything okay? I'm sensing a lot of tension."

"Everything's fine, Margo. Brady was just leaving."

"No, I'm not," Brady snapped. "I need to speak to Aspyn for a few minutes. Privately," he added.

"I think that's an excellent idea," Margo agreed, and Aspyn gasped at the betrayal. "Y'all can use the back room. I'll just lock the front door while I'm with my client."

"Margo—"

"I'm not going to have you two cluttering up my space with all that negative energy. Yours has been bad enough today. Go and finish your conversation, okay?" She smiled as she said it, but the warning was clear.

"Fine." Aspyn sighed. *No way out but through.* "Brady? This way."

Brady's wet shoes squeaked on the concrete floor of the back room that doubled as a stock and break room. Confused at the noise, Aspyn stole a glance at his feet. He was wearing some kind of sporty hiking boot. And jeans that were damp at their frayed hems. She didn't know it was possible for him to leave the house in anything other than a suit—much less on a weekday. He unbuttoned the dressy raincoat that was every inch D.C. standard-issue to reveal a sweatshirt underneath. The contrast was disconcerting, to say the least.

"This is much better," Brady said.

"Speak for yourself."

"You're obviously still angry."

"Ya think?" Aspyn leaned against a stack of boxes. "Sorry, but nothing has changed since last week. I don't like being used and lied to. So yeah, I'm still angry about it. Don't tell me you're surprised by that."

"You *are* the one person who never fails to surprise me." He sounded amused, and his humor only confused her. "I didn't realize you could carry a grudge."

"Turns out, they're not that heavy. So, yeah, I can carry this one for a while."

He snorted and pulled out a chair, offering it to her.

"Brady, no. We can't just sit and chat about this like it's business as usual or something." She stood up straight and lifted her chin. *Do not engage* was another lesson she learned from the campaign. She needed to swallow her anger and quit being so combative if she wanted through this quickly. "I do appreciate you calling Peters's office, and if it's a peace offering, I accept. We're even. No need to worry about it anymore. I don't intend on blabbing anything about you or us or the campaign to the media, so no worries there, either. I wish you well in the future, and now we can go back to our own lives." Proud of her little speech and how well she'd held it together, she straightened her spine and let the silence fall between them.

Brady lifted an eyebrow. "Are you done?"

Her balloon of pride deflated a little. "I guess."

"Good. Because *I'd* really like to talk now, and I'd like you to listen." He waited for her nod. "We'll start at the bottom and work our way up the list. Yes, I did send the information over to Kelly. I've known her since college, but I didn't call in any favors. Your work stood on its own, so if she contacted you, rest assured you had something in there that caught her eye. No, I didn't do it as a peace offering, but I *was* trying to make amends for the mess by living up to my end of our first deal. You do deserve to be heard, and Peters's office is the best recipient for your message."

Lovely. Now she felt petty as well. "Thank you, Brady, for telling me that. It means a lot to me." She pushed off the boxes and took a step toward the door.

"Not so fast. I still want to address the other part of your complaint. The personal, you-and-me part of this that's all tangled up with the nonpersonal stuff."

Ouch. The thought hurt too much. "Please believe me when I say that I really, *really* do not want to dig through that." That was the truth. She wasn't ready to be an adult about it. It was still too raw.

"Oh, but we are."

His supercilious tone destroyed her decision to be non-combative. "No, we're not."

Brady cursed and caught her arm as she tried to brush past him.

She heard the jingle and turned around as Brady removed his hand from his pocket with a sly smile. Her jaw dropped when she saw the handcuffs dangling from his finger.

"You wouldn't."

The look on Aspyn's face was priceless. "Yes, I would. I've found this is an excellent way to force someone to listen to you, and, damn it, Aspyn, I want you to listen."

"It's illegal to restrain someone. It's kidnapping."

"I didn't press charges."

"*I* didn't put handcuffs on you."

"Then don't make me put them on you. Sit." Aspyn's lips pressed into a thin, mutinous line. "Please," he added.

Shooting daggers at him the whole time, Aspyn stomped over to the table and sat. He stifled a laugh as she put her hands on either side of her thighs and eyed him with distrust.

Lily's warning hadn't prepared him for how difficult this would be—how difficult Aspyn could be—and suddenly his carefully planned statement designed to appeal to Aspyn's rationality seemed woefully inadequate. He put the handcuffs back in his pocket and some of the ire went out of Aspyn's eyes.

"I'm sorry I didn't tell you the truth about your position with the campaign. I've been in the bubble too long, and it's skewed my vision on how other people might perceive things differently than I do. No one should have their passion and enthusiasm played with like that. Call me any name you want for doing that to you. I deserve it, and you can stay mad at me about that for as long as you like. I know I can't undo it, and I'm told there's really no way to make up for stomping on someone's optimism, but I fully admit I was wrong."

Aspyn's eyebrows went up, but she didn't say anything.

Okay. Now for the hard part. "Among the many skewed perspectives I don't share with others is the separation of my personal life from everything else. When your family is public fodder, you learn to draw lines around yourself and make a clear distinction between the public you and the private you—at least in your own mind, if nothing else. My relationship with you had nothing to do with the campaign or politics or public opinion or anything else. And it never occurred to me that you—of all people—would make that connection when I didn't."

Aspyn's eyes narrowed. "What do you mean by me 'of all people'?"

"You're the one who from the get-go didn't want our relationship known at HQ or elsewhere. You were very clear on that. I assumed you keyed into that same separation of the two that I had."

"Oh. That makes sense." Her mouth twisted, and he saw more of her anger deflate. "Then that's my bad. I apologize for conflating the two and getting bent out of shape over it." She took a deep breath and smiled the fakest smile he'd ever seen on her face. "Well, I'm glad we cleared that up…" She rubbed her palms against her jeans and stood.

"Aspyn. Not so fast. I'm still not done."

"Then could you please just get to your point? This is all very fascinating, and I'm so glad you can be dispassionate about it, but I can't. I'm hurt and I'm still not over that yet."

There was the hint and *opening he needed.* "And there's my point. I understand the anger and I deserve it. But 'hurt' means there's more to this than just you feeling like I used you in some political game."

Aspyn rested her chin in her hands and rubbed her fingers across her eyes. "Fine, who needs pride anyway?" she mumbled to the tabletop. Then she sat up and looked him squarely in the eye. "I understand that I'm not good enough for you—"

That was out of left field. "What the hell…?"

"You're a Marshall. I get it. You can't really go out in public with somebody like me."

This conversation had just taken one hell of a sharp turn in the wrong direction. "Whoa, wait just a—"

"It's okay. I'm proud of who and what I am, but… You need a Jackie Kennedy. I get that. It's really okay," she rushed to assure him as his head threatened to explode. "It was just, at the time, I kinda felt like there was more… I mean, a possibility. No, that's not what I mean, either." She ran her hands through her hair and tugged at the curls.

"What do you mean?" When she didn't answer, he moved to kneel next to her chair. "Aspyn?"

"I started to think there was more to us. More than just the sex. That's *my* fault, I know, not yours—"

His heart finally started beating again as Aspyn rushed ahead, completely exonerating him from her "misunderstanding of the situation." He started to laugh.

Aspyn interrupted herself to frown at him. "I don't really see this as funny, Brady. I—"

He cut her off with a kiss, holding her until the tension began to leave her body.

"There's a lot more to us."

Her eyes were wide and soft. "R-really?"

"You are the only person I trust to know that not only will I eat quiche, I actually like it. You make me see things in a whole different light, and I realize you're the only person whose opinion of what kind of man I am matters at all to me. I hate the fact I'm sleeping alone and for the first time in my life, I'm lonely. I miss you." Aspyn's lower lip started to tremble. "You don't have to forgive me, and I'm not asking you to, but I am asking you for another chance. I need you to come back so I'm not half-dead anymore."

She blinked, and for a moment he thought he was getting through. Then she frowned. "But your family..."

Sometimes it was tough to be a Marshall. "Will adore you. Lily and Ethan and Granddad are already on your team, and the rest will follow. You're rather irresistible. And I would know, since I tried to resist you and failed." He cocked his head. "You may not like *them* very much, though..."

"I'm sure they're all lovely people, but that's not what I mean."

He wished he could make sense of this conversation. "And that would be...?"

"You've got a great career ahead of you. Someone like me... Well, I would be a liability. An embarrassment looking for a place to happen."

"If anything, you've proven 'someone like you' is an asset to the political system. And anything short of an all-out scandal isn't even enough to warrant warming up the spin machine for. We Marshalls are tough to embarrass."

"You say that now—"

Enough. "Aspyn, look at me." He cupped his hands around her cheeks and felt the dampness on her skin. "You're worrying over details and completely avoiding the main issue."

Lily hadn't been kidding at all. Not only was he having

to grovel, he was going to have to go out on the ledge first—with no guarantee she'd join him there. "I love you, Aspyn."

Aspyn couldn't breathe. Her heart was so full it squeezed all the air out of her lungs, and her blood pounded in her ears. Surely she hadn't heard him correctly. Men like Brady Marshall didn't fall in love with women like her. She lacked a pedigree, social standing, a similar belief system. It was the definition of insane.

She loved him so much it hurt to be without him, but she never dreamed he might be able to love her. At most, she'd hoped he might be looking for something a little longer than short-term, but actual *love*...

"Did you hear me, Aspyn?"

"I think so. You love me?"

"Yes. That's what I've been trying to tell you."

"Seriously?"

"Oh, for God's sake..." Brady pushed to his feet, took her chair, hauled her into his lap and kissed her until she was breathless. "I love you. I can't be any clearer than that. And I'd really appreciate it if you could end my suspense."

"You are the most frustrating man I've ever met, and I definitely couldn't have found anyone more different—or difficult—to get involved with. It's absolutely insane, but I'm in love with you." Saying it out loud seemed to change everything—making it all feel real.

Brady's grin could melt glaciers into little happy puddles. It was certainly putting a happy warmth in her chest—one that only grew when he kissed her with enough emotion it left her reeling. "Thank God," he mumbled against her neck.

A huge clap of thunder shook the building, and Aspyn

laughed. "Is that a 'you're welcome' or some kind of omen?"

"I think it's a reminder we could be on Kauai right now." He kissed her again, more playfully this time. "How quickly can you get packed?"

Happy couldn't begin to describe the feeling tumbling through her, and the look in Brady's eyes let her know she wasn't alone in those feelings. And that made it much harder to say, "I can't. My parents are in town."

That got Brady's attention. "Your parents flew back from Haiti because you—"

"No," she hurried to assure him. "Just a regular visit—although slightly brought on by recent events. They're proud of me, though. They think I'm one hell of an activist."

"You are. You changed my thinking, that's for sure. So when do I meet them?"

She nearly choked. "You want to meet my parents?" The implications of "meeting the parents" was scary enough, but *her* parents? Yikes. "You do understand what you're in for, right?"

"It seems only fair since you've met my family. Anyway, I'm rather curious about the shoes-to-tiger-habitat connection."

"I'll remind you of that later. Once they're done with you." She didn't know whether to be happy or worried, but found herself leaning toward cautiously optimistic. "I'll call them and see if they want to have lunch tomorrow—if you're free that is."

"Since I'm currently unemployed, I have all the time in the world. I'm also free tonight."

She shook her head. "No, you're not."

Brady's slow, sexy smile sent flutters through her. "Oh, what am I doing tonight, then?"

Aspyn wrapped her arms around him, savoring the feel of his body while her hands searched quickly. Brady was a second too late picking up on what she was doing, and the handcuffs were hers. She moved off his lap, perching instead on the table to examine the cuffs. "Funny you should show up with these. I'm quite intrigued by the possibilities. Always have been."

"Sweetheart, I'm game anytime you are." He frowned. "Those are for strictly recreational use only, you know, not—"

"I think I've told you all I needed to for the time being. And hopefully I won't have to resort to drastic measures to get you to listen to me in the future." She twirled them on her finger. "Would you really have cuffed me if I'd tried to walk out of here?"

He shifted uncomfortably. "It's a moot point now."

"Not to me." She lifted her right wrist and snapped the cuff on.

Brady's eyebrows went up. "Ah, Aspyn…"

She held her arm out, dangling the other empty cuff as a dare. Without missing a beat, Brady slipped his wrist in and it *snicked* shut. "Hmm, this feels oddly familiar."

"But this won't." Aspyn slid off the table and straddled him in the chair. "Now, is there something you want to tell me?" she asked as she put her mouth on his neck and nipped gently.

"Yeah," Brady whispered. "I don't have the keys."

EPILOGUE

"I CAN'T believe I let you talk me into this." Aspyn paced beside Brady, stopping every so often to peek around the door at the guests eyeballing each other warily across the aisle.

"The wedding? It took me over a year to get you to this point. It's not like we're rushing into anything," he teased. Aspyn hadn't been kidding about her philosophical objections to marriage. He was now ready to manage any campaign out there—*nothing* could be harder than the campaign to get Aspyn to agree to marry him. She'd moved into his life in every possible way, but getting her to the altar… Even Nana had come to accept the idea that her future great-grandchildren would be born out of wedlock before Aspyn had a complete change of mind.

"We should have eloped. This is going to be a disaster."

"No chance. My grandmother would never allow a Marshall wedding to be less than perfect—even if you did only give her a month to put it together." Aspyn had finally said "yes" at Thanksgiving and declared she wanted a Christmas wedding. Knowing Aspyn, she'd timed it this way in the hope the general holiday madness would have led their wedding to be a smaller, more low-key affair.

He'd wondered how Aspyn had managed to be a part

of his family for over a year and not realized there was no chance in hell Nana would let this wedding be small or low-key no matter how quickly it had to be planned. Nana made things happen.

Aspyn cut her eyes at him. "Your grandmother has never planned a wedding where a protest march could break out at any second. There are nine current or former members of Congress in there—not even counting the ones in your bloodline. Hell, your entire side of the aisle has Capitol Hill parking passes."

"And your side of the aisle just marches on Washington on occasion."

Aspyn spun and the small silver bells attached to her bouquet jingled. "Make jokes. Go ahead. When our first dance is to 'We Shall Overcome' because they've staged an impromptu sit-in, don't blame me."

"Breathe, Aspyn. It's going to be fine."

"Hoping for a Christmas miracle, are you?"

"Hey, you're standing here in a wedding dress. I'd call that pretty miraculous." Aspyn smacked him halfheartedly. He adjusted the greenery in her hair, tucking in a curl that had come loose during her pacing. "You look beautiful, you know."

She took a deep breath and exhaled slowly. "Thank you."

"And if they get too rowdy, I have these." He pulled the handcuffs out of his pocket.

"You brought handcuffs to our *wedding*?" she whispered, frantically looking around for witnesses. Then she snatched them out of his hand and shoved them back in his pocket.

"Just wanted to be prepared in case you got cold feet."

"My feet are toasty warm, thanks very much. I'm not backing out now."

Safe in the knowledge he was almost home free, Brady let himself ask the question he'd been keeping to himself the last few weeks. "What *did* finally make you change your mind?"

She smiled up at him. "Because I chose you. Not only for today, but every day for the rest of my life. And I want everyone to know that." The smile took on an edge as she shrugged. "Either that, or your mainstream, establishment values have totally corrupted me," she teased.

He laughed out loud. "Whatever works. I don't care how or why as long as you make it down that aisle to say 'I do.'"

Aspyn grinned and rose up on her tiptoes to kiss him. "Besides," she added, "I didn't know what else to get you for Christmas. You're impossible to shop for, you know."

"I guess I'll return your present then. It's a pity." He shook his head. "You would have loved it."

"I don't need another present." Aspyn wrapped her arms around his waist and leaned into him. "I have you, and I know I love that."

He pulled her closer and lowered his head so their lips were only inches apart. "Well, when you put it that way…"

"Can't you two wait a few more minutes until you're legal?" Finn rounded the corner with Ethan and Lily on his heels.

"What are you two doing?" Lily huffed disapprovingly at them. "You're not supposed to see each other before the wedding." She turned to Finn and frowned. "*You* were supposed to be keeping an eye on him."

"I only turned my back for a minute. It's not my fault

he can't leave her alone." Finn winked at Aspyn. "Not that I blame him at all, of course."

"First Lily and now Aspyn?" Ethan elbowed his younger brother. "Why don't you find your own girl and leave ours alone."

"I think that's an excellent idea, Finn." Nana's voice caused them all to jump like guilty teenagers, and they turned to see Nana and the Breedloves waiting next to the door.

Finn frowned before throwing an elbow into Ethan with a mumbled, "Thanks." Brady bit back a laugh. Like Nana needed any more reason to harp on Finn—with first Ethan and now him getting married, there would be nowhere for Finn to hide now.

Nana sent a sharp look in their direction. "Behave, you two," she warned. "Go find your grandfather and take your places. Lily, you, too. Brady, get your hands off Aspyn and go with your brothers."

Aspyn was biting back a smile of her own. Aware of his audience, Brady settled for dropping a chaste kiss on Aspyn's cheek. "See you in a minute."

He left her to the fussing of her parents, who didn't seem to have any problem with Aspyn doing something so "establishment" or "conformist" as getting married. In fact, her father had mentioned something last night about him and Lydia possibly making it legal after thirty-two years. He couldn't wait to see Aspyn's reaction to *that* little nugget of information.

His chuckle was abruptly cut off by Nana's crisp and horrified "Brady Mason Marshall." *She'd noticed.* After the whole no-tie debacle, he'd kept the rest of his wardrobe choices to himself, holding on to the vain hope she wouldn't notice until it was too late. No such luck. Nana noticed *everything*.

"What on earth are you *wearing*?"

Brady took her arm gently and led her down the aisle. She wouldn't make a scene in front of the guests. "You see, Nana, there are these wild tiger habitats…"

Aspyn had to hand it to Regina Marshall. The woman could plan a wedding. Oh, there was an official wedding planner around here somewhere, but Aspyn knew who was really pulling the strings.

The music changed—giving Aspyn her cue—but she took a second just to take it all in. While she'd originally hoped for something small with minimal fuss, she was now glad that Brady's grandmother had insisted on pulling out all the stops. A friend of their family's had opened their summer house for her wedding, giving the gathering an intimate feel—even with over a hundred guests in attendance. Floor-to-ceiling windows faced Chesapeake Bay, and the weak wintery sunshine managed to sparkle on the water, providing a magical backdrop to Brady standing there next to the judge he'd just helped get reelected.

In a way, she wished she had been able to have the wedding on the beach, with the sand between her toes and the sunshine in her face, but waiting another six months for the weather to cooperate wasn't an option. Instead they'd managed to bring the outdoors in, and the smell of evergreens filled her nose. The room had a festive winter feel, without looking too Christmassy; it was elegant without being formal and stiff.

The wedding was an odd compromise between the mainstream and the fringe—just like she and Brady. She never dreamed she'd get married at all, much less to someone like him. But Brady was the yin to her yang; an opposite that made her complete. It kept things interesting, yet comfortable.

And while her connection to the Marshall family had opened all kinds of doors to her, they weren't along the path she'd planned because there were ethical problems of lobbying to people you were about to be related to by marriage. But, if she'd learned anything at all from being with Brady, it was the importance of the bigger picture. Changing the approach wasn't bad as long as the goal stayed in sight.

Right now, her goal was at the end of a long red carpet that ran between factions so at odds they almost needed treaties and accords just to get them in the same room. It was funny: she'd been so worried all morning about a riot breaking out, but now her perspective shifted to more important things.

Today was her wedding day, and she wanted nothing more than to marry Brady and tie that knot just as tight as it could possibly go.

Brady raised an eyebrow at her, and Aspyn realized she'd been standing there a moment too long. Somehow she didn't doubt Brady would come up the aisle and hand-cuff her if she didn't get moving soon. *That* would definitely liven things up. He visibly relaxed once she took a step in his direction.

She hadn't been kidding when she told Brady she already had what she wanted for Christmas. She, Aspyn Breedlove—soon-to-be-Marshall—had somehow ended up getting everything she'd *never* wanted in life. That was one heck of a surprise present.

The even bigger surprise? She couldn't be happier.

* * * * *

My wish list for next month's titles...

In stores from 18th November 2011:

❏ Jewel in His Crown – Lynne Graham

❏ Once a Ferrara Wife... – Sarah Morgan

❏ In Bed with a Stranger – India Grey

❏ The Call of the Desert – Abby Green

❏ How to Win the Dating War – Aimee Carson

In stores from 2nd December 2011:

❏ The Man Every Woman Wants – Miranda Lee

❏ Not Fit for a King? – Jane Porter

❏ In a Storm of Scandal – Kim Lawrence

❏ Playing His Dangerous Game – Tina Duncan

❏ Acquired: The CEO's Small-Town Bride – Catherine Mann

Available at WHSmith, Tesco, Asda, Eason, Amazon and Apple

1111/0

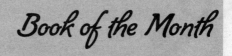

MILLS & BOON Book Club

2 Free Books!

Get your free books now at

www.millsandboon.co.uk/freebookoffer

Or fill in the form below and post it back to us

THE MILLS & BOON® BOOK CLUB™—HERE'S HOW IT WORKS: Accepting your free books places you under no obligation to buy anything. You may keep the books and return the despatch note marked 'Cancel'. If we do not hear from you, about a month later we'll send you 4 brand-new stories from the Modern™ series priced at £3.30* each. There is no extra charge for post and packaging. You may cancel at any time, otherwise we will send you 4 stories a month which you may purchase or return to us—the choice is yours. *Terms and prices subject to change without notice. Offer valid in UK only. Applicants must be 18 or over. Offer expires 28th February 2012. **For full terms and conditions, please go to www.millsandboon.co.uk/termsandconditions**

Mrs/Miss/Ms/Mr (please circle) _____

First Name _____

Surname _____

Address _____

_____

Postcode _____

E-mail _____

Send this completed page to: Mills & Boon Book Club, Free Book Offer, FREEPOST NAT 10298, Richmond, Surrey, TW9 1BR

Find out more at
www.millsandboon.co.uk/freebookoffer

Visit us Online

0611/P1ZEE

Special Offers

Every month we put together collections and longer reads written by your favourite authors.

Here are some of next month's highlights— and don't miss our fabulous discount online!

that Christmas *Feeling*
Debbie Macomber
SHERRYL WOODS · ROBYN CARR

On sale 18th November

DIANA PALMER
Christmas Cowboy

On sale 18th November

ROYAL *Christmas*
KATE HEWITT · SUSAN MALLERY · HELEN BETTS

On sale 18th November

Save 20%
on all Special Releases

Mills & Boon® Online

Discover more romance at
www.millsandboon.co.uk

- 🌹 **FREE** online reads
- 🌹 **Books** up to one month before shops
- 🌹 **Browse our books** before you buy

...and much more!

For exclusive competitions and instant updates:

 Like us on **facebook.com/romancehq**

 Follow us on **twitter.com/millsandboonuk**

 Join us on **community.millsandboon.co.uk**

Visit us Online Sign up for our FREE eNewsletter at **www.millsandboon.co.uk**